J G White was born and raised in London and the South East. He served in the Royal Marines during the 1960s and saw active service in Borneo at the time of the Brunei Rebellion. He now lives in Nottingham where he taught for many years.

# OPERATION
SAINT GEORGE

To KS with much love

J. G. White

# OPERATION SAINT GEORGE

AUSTIN MACAULEY
PUBLISHERS LTD.

Copyright © J. G. White

The right of J. G. White to be identified as author of this work has been asserted by him in accordance with section 77 and 78 of the Copyright, Designs and Patents Act 1988.

All rights reserved. No part of this publication may be reproduced, stored in a retrieval system, or transmitted in any form or by any means, electronic, mechanical, photocopying, recording, or otherwise, without the prior permission of the publishers.

Any person who commits any unauthorized act in relation to this publication may be liable to criminal prosecution and civil claims for damages.

A CIP catalogue record for this title is available from the British Library.

ISBN 9781849633390

www.austinmacauley.com

First Published (2013)
Austin Macauley Publishers Ltd.
25 Canada Square
Canary Wharf
London
E14 5LB

Printed and Bound in Great Britain

This book is respectfully dedicated to all those "Royals" who, wherever they were serving in the world, undertook some thankless task at the behest of others; and for whatever reason failed to receive the recognition they truly and rightfully deserved.

"A Royal Marines Commando is always expected to achieve the impossible"

> HRH Prince Philip
> Captain General
> 29 November 1952

# PROLOGUE

Joseph Conrad once said, "Inside the heart of every man there is a desire to set down what is true."

It was only by a chance encounter whilst sailing on the River Orwell in Suffolk that the events told in this book came to light and subsequently allowed this story to be told publicly for the first time.

Hopefully you the reader will be as intrigued as I was by these events, which in themselves are quite extraordinary, but also by the fact that for nearly forty-five years this story has remained completely locked away. It has been hidden not only from the general public, but also from the annals of the Royal Marines' own history, due to the then government imposing a complete "most secret" on the whole affair.

It is a fact that the Royal Marines have an unusual sense of humour, which many outside of their Corps do not really understand; they are also great story tellers. Marines are also extremely loyal, not only to each other but also to their Corps, even after they have left the service. They will always help each other out; it is part of the tradition of being a "Royal": once a Royal Marine always a Royal Marine.

I am therefore deeply indebted to a number of Marines past and present who have helped me with research for this book, too many to list here, and also to some other people who for their own reasons still wish to avoid the public eye. However, to one person in particular I am most grateful for the help given to me, Mr Alan John Dacre of Woodbridge, Suffolk, and for the many hours we spent together as one old "Royal" to another, remembering our days in the Corps.

To help those readers with no experience of the Royal Marines, I have put together a glossary at the back of the book, which I hope goes some way to help understand this unique Corps and the men who serve in it.


JG White

# PART ONE

*Vero Nihil Verius*

(nothing truer than the truth)

# ROYAL NAVY AND ROYAL MARINES SERVICE RECORD (R141)
## Training and Employment History

Official No.: Chatham/X 06821 Rank: Mne 1$^{st}$ Class
Surname: DACRE Christian Name(s): Alan John

| Unit or Ship | Rank | Trade/Tech Qual of SQ | Capacity in which employed | Dates (from-to) | Remarks as to professional/instructional ability, special qualifications, awards, characteristics, etc. | Signature of Head of Dept., etc. |
|---|---|---|---|---|---|---|
| RM Depot | Mne 2nd | - | Recruit | Feb 39- Sept 39 | Best all round recruit in his squad. Awarded King's Badge. Marksman | *J Bateson* Capt. RM |
| Chatham Division | Mne 2nd | - | Trained Soldier | Sep 30- May 40 | Further training in Royal Marines Company. Excellent potential. | *V Taylor* Capt RM |
| RM Company | Mne 1st | - | Trained Soldier | May 40 – Dec 41 | Underage; unable to go to France with Company. Volunteered for small boats; to Dunkirk on Gypsey Rose. Awarded Legion d'Honneur. Detached duties London. | *H Derry* Major RM OC Coy |
| Training School | Mne 1st | - | Cdo Training | Feb 42- Aug 42 | Commando training at Deal, Isle of Wight and Acknercarry Scotland. An outstanding Marine. Awarded 1$^{st}$ Service stripe. | *J Graham* Capt RM |
| Cdo RM | Mne 1st | - | RM Cdo | May 42- Dec 42 | Took part in Dieppe raid, mentioned in dispatches. Awarded MM. Refused promotion. Awarded Green Beret and NGS | *G Ellis* Captain and OC |
| RMB Eastney | Mne 1st | - | Swimmer/ Canoeist training | Jan 43- April 43 | 3 months SBS training, passed out top of his course. Refused promotion. | *P Naylor* Capt RM |
| 48 Cdo RM | Mne 1st | SC | Cdo | May 43- Sept 45 | D-Day landings, awarded DCM and bar to MM. Temporary field promotions to sergeant and captain. Reverted to marine in 1945. Born leader of men. Awarded 2$^{nd}$ Service stripe | *JL Moulton* Lt Col RM Commanding Officer |
| Infantry School RM | Mne 1st | SC | Sniper and Field craft Course | Oct 45 –Jan 46 | Top of his course. A very creditable performance | *R Paul* Major RM |
| 3 Cdo Bde RM | Mne 1st | SC | Special Boat Section | Jan 46- Jan 48 | IS duties in Hong Kong with No. 6 SBS. Mentioned in Dispatches. Refused promotion. | *I Burton* Capt RM |
| 3 Cdo Bde RM | Mne 1st | SC | SBS Unit | Feb 48- | Mediterranean and Middle East operations. | *A Mercer* Capt & Adjt |

| | | | | Jan 50 | Outstanding team member. Awarded 3rd Service stripe. | RM |
|---|---|---|---|---|---|---|
| 41 Ind Cdo RM | Mne 1st | SC | SC attached to 41 Cdo Part of USA 1st Marine Division | Jan 50-Jan 52 | Served with distinction. Mentioned in dispatches, bar to MM and Congressional Medal of Honour (USA). | *D Dilnot* Major RM |
| 40 Cdo RM | Mne 1st | SC | Commando | Feb 52-May 54 | Palestine and Suez Canal. An outstanding marine. Bar to DCM. Awarded Long Service & Good Conduct Medal. | *JV Grealy* Capt RM |
| 3 CDO Bde RM | Mne 1st | SC | SBS Unit | Jun 54-Jan 56 | No. 6 SBS Unit on anti-terrorist duties. Made a major contribution. MID | *M Bussey* Capt RM |
| JSWAC Poole | Mne 1st | SC | Instructor | Feb56-Dec 59 | Has initiative, intelligence and drive. Refused promotion. | *C Copping* Capt & Adjt RM |
| Plymouth Group Stonehouse Barracks | Mne 1st | SC | Instructor | Dec 59-June 61 | An unusually interesting and intelligent marine. Has successfully assumed many responsibilities. Refused Promotion. | *R Peacock* Major RM OC |
| 43 Cdo RM | Mne 1st | SC | Recce Troop | Jul 61-March 62 | A most efficient, effective and knowledgeable member of the Troop. His experience has been a major factor in the development of this team. | *E Hayes* Major RM OC |
| Depot RM | Mne 1st | SC | I/C Pioneer Section | Mar 62-May 62 | For discharge and release after 22 years honourable service. A natural leader of men, has the ability to undertake any task regardless of difficulty and sees it through to the end. | *G Ellis* Brigadier RM Commandant |

**ENGLAND 1962**

# 1

IT was an unusually warm and sunny afternoon that day in March. A slight breeze drifted across from the seafront and blew silently along the small side road that led to the barrack gates. A Royal Marines sentry stood silent and perfectly still, his dark blue uniform making a sharp contrast to the immaculate white belt and cross-strap, the brasses gleaming in the sun. Motionless he watched the breeze create tiny eddies of dust in the roadside gutter. A very fine layer, almost invisible to the naked eye, settled on his highly polished boots. Only half an hour to go before his relief was due, he thought.

The sentry's attention was drawn to an oncoming figure. He squinted against the glare of the sun from beneath his white peaked cap. Walking towards him with a purposeful step was a man carrying a kit bag under one arm and in the other a beige grip, so beloved by sailors and marines alike. The sentry studied the stranger carefully; blazer with corps badge and tie to match, grey flannels well pressed and black shoes. Height about six foot, quite broad in the shoulders, age difficult to tell, anywhere between thirty and forty years old. Nevertheless he looked fit, very fit. Clearly a marine who had seen some service.

"Good morning, Corporal." The marine had dropped his bags lightly, addressing the sentry correctly, having seen the single stripe, gold on red on his right arm. He reached into his blazer pocket and produced a blue Royal Navy identity card. The corporal took it, looked first at the photograph then at the face.

The face was older. Name, rank and number were all quickly scanned and assimilated. Back to the name, Dacre AJ,

Marine First Class, DOB 01.08.21. Regimental Number Chatham/X 06821.

The corporal looked at the marine. "Welcome back Royal," he said with just a hint of a smile that touched the corners of his mouth. "Been a while, has it?"

"Not since 1942," the marine replied. He remembered that year all too vividly, that bleak month of February when the first Royal Marine Commandos gathered at Deal. They were faced with no easy task: the Army Commandos ignored them, the Corps was generally against them and then there were the Germans.

"The Depot has changed a bit since then, but still producing the goods." The corporal hesitated slightly. "Sorry I can't let you in by this gate, you'll have to go around to the guardroom and report there. Go up the gravel drive, past where those pioneers are supposed to be working, turn right at the road, the guardroom is about a hundred yards down on the right hand side, you can't miss it. Report to the guard commander, he'll sign you in and tell you where to go next."

Dacre thanked him, picked up his bags and moved off. The corporal watched him go, so he thought that's Dacre AJ, a legend in his own time so they say, I wonder what he is doing here? The corporal noticed that the bottom of the marine's kit bag was painted red and yellow with the number 43 stencilled on it.

Although the marine walked quickly along the gravel drive, the seasoned observer would have noticed that despite being laden with all of his kit, his step was extremely light, so much so that he barely raised any dust. To his right was a large and solid looking high wall beyond which was the barrack's parade ground. On his left the backs and gardens of the shops that overlooked the sea front and promenade. Some were neat and tidy, others were unkempt; all were clearly visible through the wrought iron railings, which fenced off the gardens from the gravel drive. Midway he passed a narrow alleyway which cut down between the shops to the main road. Dacre could just glimpse the beach and the sea beyond, for which Deal and Walmer were justly famous as a holiday destination.

Dacre AJ approached the small group of marines who were supposedly working. The corporal had been right. At first glance they appeared to be busy, to the more discerning eye they were clearly skiving! A couple of marines had crafty cigarettes on the go, cupped in their hands so as not to be seen. There were four marines in all, together with a small hand-drawn cart full of spades and brooms, the tools of their trade. The cart also contained evidence of a not very productive morning, just a handful of weeds. One marine, who seemed younger than the others, was on his hands and knees trying to pull a particularly large stubborn weed from against the wall, while the others looked on, encouraging him with much humour and vulgarity.

As Dacre AJ passed them, they fell silent. He walked on, taking in every, nothing missed, even a face that he recognised from the past. Marines like this were given the title of "Pioneers". They were used to keeping the barracks clean and tidy. Not the best of jobs, thought Dacre, but someone had to do it. Often pioneers were men waiting to go outside, their time almost up in the Corps, or marines who, for whatever reason, just didn't fit in.

The little group watched in silence as Dacre reached the end of the drive and turned right.
"Bloody hell!" said one of them. "I know him!"
"What's up Pincher?" said another marine looking questioningly at Marine James Martin, known to all as "Pincher."
"That's Dacre AJ, that's who that is!"
"Fucking hell!" said another. "What's he doing here?"
"Someone is in for it!" said the third marine.
"Who the hell is Dacre AJ?" said the fourth and youngest marine.
"Don't be a wanker," said Pincher Martin. "Everyone knows about him!"
"Well, I don't" said the young marine. One of the others looked at his watch.

"Come on, it's nearly time for stand easy, let's get a wet of tea over in the NAAFI and we'll tell you all about him, that'll improve your knowledge of real Corps history by at least a hundred and ten percent."

Walking down the gravel drive Dacre AJ could clearly see the vast parade ground to his right with its distinctive undulating humps caused by the underground drainage system. A squad of recruits were drilling under the watchful eye of their drill instructor. Even after all these years it hadn't changed that much, except for a new three-story building, unfamiliar to him. Memories of his basic training back in 1939, when a marine was a marine, began to surface. He deliberately pushed them away, it was too long ago and too much water had flowed under the bridge since then. To his left was a short road that led down to an old chapel, now obviously used as a practice space for Royal Marine Bandsmen, since he could hear the strains of some march or other, and, although he couldn't quite place the tune, he started to hum the words 'isn't it a pity she'd only one titty to feed the baby on.' With amazing clarity he suddenly remembered that his Drill Sergeant used to quietly sing this to his own recruit squad, whilst they and the other squads were doing their weekly march through the town.

At the main road he paused before turning right. On the opposite side of the road was a pub called the 'Green Beret.' What had it been called in his day? He couldn't remember. Passing the gates to South Barracks, he saw a squad of recruits in PE order being marched out, wearing their battledress tops with their Royal Marines flashes, long white shorts and plimsolls and their blue berets with the distinctive red patch behind the cap badge. Their instructor was urging them to beat with their left foot as they marched. Dacre AJ smiled to himself, some things never change, and they weren't too bad for beginners.

The sentry on duty at the main gate waved him towards the guardroom, almost as if he was directing traffic. It was as Dacre AJ remembered it; a very large room with high windows that you couldn't see out of, tables, chairs and bunk beds for the night guard and fire piquet, who were usually recruits. Smaller rooms with very heavy doors, used as holding cells, were ranged along one wall. A passageway led out to an internal courtyard and the heads. The deck was a pale brown lino, well-polished, the whole place was immaculately painted and gleaming, fire buckets standing neatly in a row. In the centre of the room stood a large cast iron stove and chimney, freshly blackened and shining with a neatly painted white brick surround. Nothing out of place, everything as it should be.

The guardroom office was directly in front of Dacre AJ as he went in. The Guard Commander, a corporal was sitting behind a large well-ordered desk. The Duty Sergeant stood behind him with his back to the fireplace. Despite the warmth outside there was a fire in the grate, which gave off a distinctive smell of burning coke. Like the outer room, the office was marine clean and tidy, even the fireplace was spotless. Both NCOs were wearing blue uniforms, number three dress, indicated by their red badges of rank. Dacre AJ halted in front of the desk, placed his bags on the floor and handed over his ID card and travel orders to the corporal. He then stood to attention, his thumbs in line with the seams of his trousers. He knew the routine and what was expected of him. The corporal took his time checking the documents and then made an entry into a large ledger in front of him. He studied the marine's ID card carefully and then turned and passed it to the sergeant who glanced at it and passed it back to Dacre AJ.

" Go across the barrack road outside to 'A' block and report to the HQ Company Sergeant Major, he's expecting you."

"Thank you, Corporal." Dacre AJ picked up his bags, nodded to the sergeant, turned about smartly and marched out.

The corporal turned to look at his sergeant for a moment. "So that's the famous Dacre is it, he doesn't look so much."

"No, he doesn't," replied the sergeant. "That's where most people make the mistake."

Back in the sunlight Dacre AJ walked quickly across to HQ Company building. As he did so, he passed a vehicle park full of land rovers and three-ton trucks. Beyond them he could just see the outline of the Globe and Laurel Theatre which also doubled up as the camp cinema. The company office was on the ground floor, where a marine clerk was busily typing. He looked up as the marine entered the office and without bothering to stop shouted out "Sergeant Major!" The name plate on the door said *QMS R Collins RM MM.* The sergeant major stepped out, a big man in many ways with a large moustache and an even larger stomach.

"Where the bloody hell have you been?" he bellowed. "I sent transport to the railway station to collect you hours ago! Well?"

Dacre AJ was somewhat taken aback by this verbal onslaught, but true to his nature he remained calm and unfazed.

"I'm sorry, Sergeant Major; I came by bus from Canterbury."

The Sergeant Major looked at him for a moment. "What the bloody hell were you doing in Canterbury?"

The company clerk had by this time stopped typing and was clearly enjoying the exchange; he had a somewhat bemused expression on his face, after all very few people had ever got the better of his boss.

"Actually Sergeant Major, I spent a long weekend in Whitstable having travelled up from Plymouth by car. I have a small house in Tankerton. I left my car there and came by bus to Canterbury and then on to here. You'll see from my travel orders that it includes a weekend pass."

The Sergeant Major made a sound resembling a snort: he had clearly been outmanoeuvred this time. The clerk busied himself shuffling some papers in order to hide his grin, this had been a first and oh so well done!

"Right then, leave your gear here, the Company Commander will see you now, as you are, follow me." Dacre AJ turned to follow and, as he did so, the clerk leaned across and whispered, "Don't for heaven's sake smile."

The Sergeant Major had already knocked and entered the Company Commander's office. "Attention! Quick march, halt, do not salute! Marine Dacre AJ," he barked out, "just arrived from 43 Commando RM Plymouth, Sir!" Dacre stood stiffly to attention, looking straight ahead, not even blinking.

"Thank you, Sergeant Major." The officer behind the desk looked up. "Stand at ease," he said. Dacre AJ looked down at him, the name plate on the desk said *Captain W Dewar RM MC.*

"Well Dacre, welcome back to The Depot. There'll have been a few changes since you were last here, when was it?" He glanced down at the contents of a buff-coloured folder. "Ah yes 1942. However, why you are here is something of a mystery to me. You're due to go outside in May having completed your twenty-two years of service, is that correct?" He looked up at the marine and smiled. Dacre AJ very nearly smiled back, but just in time remembered the clerk's warning.

"Yes Sir, that is correct."

Captain Dewar continued, "Normally you would have been discharged in Plymouth, and yet here you are on loan to us, not even transferred. It's all very irregular, isn't it, Sergeant Major?"

"As you say Sir, all very irregular." Dacre AJ remained silent; he knew when to keep quiet.

"You're to be on the Commanding Officer's orderly room tomorrow morning at 0900 hours. Any questions?"

"No Sir!"

"That's all then, I think Sergeant Major, carry on."

"Sir! Attention! About turn, quick march, report to my office immediately."


"Right then Dacre, you've got the rest of the afternoon to settle in. Tomorrow's rig of the day will be battledress, white belt and beret, and make sure you wear parade boots, not SVs. The second-in-command has a thing about boots, so be warned. The scribes in the office will sort you out a pit." With that he was gone. The company clerk gave him his room number, top floor, room three. Collecting his belongings Dacre AJ made his way up the well-worn stone stairs to the top of the building. This was a typical barrack block, built over two hundred years ago during the Napoleonic period, well before the RMLI moved to Deal and developed The Depot as their training centre. Trudging up the stairs Dacre AJ tried to remember his days here as a recruit; he and his squad mates had been billeted in a building just like this one, but it was all a bit hazy, time he supposed.

# 2

OPENING the barrack door Dacre AJ was greeted by an overpowering smell of floor polish and fresh paint. This was a room typical of most Royal Marine's barracks. It was big enough to hold eight iron bedsteads; each bed space had a metal locker. In the centre of the room was a table, the wooden top scrubbed immaculately white, with chairs pushed neatly under. Each bed had the usual mattress with a perfectly squared away bed-pack. On the floor at the foot of each bed was the usual row of well-polished boots and shoes. The wood block floor, surely a later addition, was highly polished, as was the metal spittoon which acted as a gash bucket. Nothing out of place, thought Dacre AJ, these marines know what they are about.

There were two vacant beds, Dacre AJ chose the one in the right corner, next to a window. Looking out, he could clearly see the large new block opposite, presumably for the recruits, junior marines and trainee musicians. It hadn't been there in his day. He also had a fine view of the parade ground and beyond it the drill shed, almost as big as an aircraft hangar. He unpacked his gear and set up his locker, then made up his bed ready for the evening. From his grip he took out his parade boots, removed the protective covering from the toe caps. They had travelled well and wouldn't need much work on them in order to bring them up to scratch. Just time to get his battledress pressed, he thought. Making his way downstairs he called in at the company office just to verify the location of the pressing shop. Suitably informed, he made his way across the road and past the NAFFI block; on the spur of the moment he went inside to buy another jar of white Blanco. Inside, the shop was selling all the usual sort of things that recruits might need: polish, dusters, toothpaste and so on. In addition, there was a fresh bar serving milk, orange juice and tea and coffee. Dacre AJ noticed that high up on the walls there were paintings of various Corps battles: Belle Isle, Gibraltar, Zeebrugge and Salerno. Clearly Corps history was still high on the agenda. He made his purchase and then walked quickly past the Trained Soldiers wet canteen and the main entrance to the dining hall to the pressing shop, which as it turned out was opposite the old chapel he had passed earlier in the day. He was lucky, he didn't have long to wait, and fifteen minutes later Dacre AJ was back in his room with a uniform that was freshly pressed with razor sharp creases.

Dacre AJ spent the next twenty minutes or so cleaning his white belt and the brasses, then carefully whitening the badges on his battledress jacket. Next came his boots. Using a little bit of black shoe polish, cold water and some cotton wool he gently bulled up the toe caps of his boots until they were gleaming like mirrors. The underneath of the boots were given a quick blackening and then buffed up, studs and all. Dacre AJ took out his commando Green Beret, once despised because of its colour, but now revered almost everywhere in the world. He took off his brass badge and gave it a good clean – most of the detail had been worn away with the constant polishing over the years. He knew that many marines had changed to the new stay bright badges. At present they were still optional, so he chose to keep his old badge; he guessed it would see his time out in the Corps. Before replacing the badge, he gave the holding pin a quick clean; old habits die hard he thought.

He was just finishing ironing his shirt and tie when the barrack room door crashed opened and in came four very noisy marines. They stopped dead in their tracks. It was not clear who was the more surprised. Dacre AJ immediately recognised them as the group of pioneers he had seen earlier. James Martin better known as 'Pincher' stepped forward with his hand held out.

"AJ, it's been a while."

They shook hands. The two had not really been friends, more acquaintances. They had met some years ago when Martin had been undergoing his swimmer – canoeists course at Poole. Dacre

AJ had been at the Amphibious Training Centre at the same time on a refresher course. Martin had finished top of his course, but later failed the psychological tests.

"Good to see you Pincher, how are things with you?"

"Okay!" said Martin rather sullenly, "I get by." There was a slight pause. "The bastards failed me, you know, said I had the wrong attitude. Fuck them, what do they know?" Dacre AJ shrugged in a non-committal way.

"I heard on the grapevine. That's tough."

Pincher Martin looked around the room. The other marines had gone to their bed spaces and were getting changed. Pincher spoke first. "Let me introduce you to the lads. Over here in the blue corner we have Marine Peter Woods, ' Timber' to you and me from the East End of London, but as he will constantly tell you, not a Cockney." Woods came across the room to shake hands. Martin continued. "He's a cocky bugger though, always fighting, in and out of DQs like a yo-yo. Also trained as a medical orderly, useful if you get a splinter in your arse or a dose of the clap! Oh yes, and his nine years are coming up this October and he can't wait to get out. Next we have Marine Arthur Fagin, he generally answers to 'Art', he's from Nottingham, but we don't hold that against him. He was a Corporal PTI down at Lympstone, taught the unarmed combat part of the commando course until he went AWOL and nearly half-killed his wife's boyfriend. Got eighteen months in Portsmouth DQs and came out smiling. They should have kicked him out, but didn't for some strange reason." Fagin looked up and nodded a greeting.

"This youngster over here is Marine Harry Taylor, known as 'Tubby' for obvious reasons. Comes from a long line of Royals, way back to the dot! Tubby was a ship's marine, landing craft, but got sent ashore because he kept getting sea sick. Ain't that right?" Taylor looked embarrassed. "Yeh, something like that." Martin continued.

"Tubby's great talent is that he is a fantastic scrounger, he can get you almost anything given half a chance. Dacre AJ nodded a greeting, Taylor looked away.

"Those two empty pits belong to Marines Preece and Day. At the moment they are both in DQs here in the barracks doing fourteen days a piece for being drunk and disorderly. Day is a 'Geordie' from Newcastle and Preece is from Birmingham.

Geordie was an Assault Engineer but lost his nerve handling explosives, something he doesn't talk about. Brum Preece on the other hand is a bloody good marine when sober, none better. But after a couple of drinks can lose it and has been known to go berserk." From the far corner of the room Tubby Taylor sniggered and said,

"Brum was so drunk that when they put him in the cells, and it took half a dozen provosts to do just that, he began shaking the cell door off its hinges, so much so they had to get the 'chippy' out of bed to nail it up!"

Martin looked at Taylor, "Thanks for that, you wanker! So AJ that's us lot, all a bit washed up as you can see. What about you, what the fuck are you doing here?"

Dacre AJ paused before answering. "I'm not really sure why I am here. I am due to go outside in May, my twenty-two is up then. I'm with 43 Commando at the present and should be on my way to Aden with all the others. Instead I find myself fast tracked to here. Even the Company Commander doesn't know why. I'm seeing the CO in the morning, so I should find out then. It's all a bit of a mystery really."

At that moment, the duty bugler sounded the call for the evening meal.

"Come on," said Pincher, "this will be an experience you won't forget, there's a new squad in!"

# 3

THE dining hall was very large; it could easily seat about three hundred men comfortably. The right hand side had been sectioned off for the corporals and trained soldiers. The food was good and wholesome and there was plenty of it. Dacre AJ and the little group of pioneers sat at a table in a corner out of the way. He was taking in the whole experience; it had been a long time since he had been in a training barracks and it had been nothing like this. The others were watching him with interest.

Dacre AJ suddenly said, "I need a mug of tea." As he went to stand up, Timber Woods reached over and firmly held his arm to the table.

"Don't!" he said. "We think they put Bromide in the tea, stops the recruits from getting too randy."

"Some of us reckon it gets in our tea as well," said Tubby Taylor.

Dacre AJ looked at them both and then at the others who were all nodding.

"Well, I wouldn't want it to ruin my love life, such as it is, now, would I?"


Suddenly the chatter and noise in the dining hall had ceased. A group of about forty brand new recruits had been ushered in for their first meal. Many of them weren't yet in full uniform, civilian shirts could be seen underneath their fatigues. They looked totally lost, not sure what to do or where to go, or indeed what was expected of them. Each one stood holding his eating irons and his tin mug, nervously waiting for some guidance. Then, as if by some unseen command, every man in the dining hall began to hammer their knives and forks on the table tops in perfect unison, the sound as one, getting louder and louder, and rising to a deafening thunder. Looks of fear and trepidation spread across the faces of the new recruits. The welcome, for that is what it was, lasted for no more than a minute or so. Then the recruits' squad instructor stepped into the hall. He stood perfectly still, his pace stick under his right arm, immaculate in his best blue uniform. He waited. Then, as if by a command, the hammering stopped.

Pincher Martin looked at Dacre AJ and shrugged. "It's okay, a tradition, all new boys get that. Next week they'll be doing it to some other poor sods. We even join in sometimes, it's good for a laugh."

Fagin stood up. "Come on, let's get a decent cup of tea, then later we can have a couple of pints in the wet canteen."

As they were leaving, Dacre AJ stopped and looked across the hall towards the washing-up area used by the recruits. "Who's the big guy behind the counter?"

"That's John West, the CO's driver. He comes in here to help out sometimes, training for the Olympics, discus, I think," said Pincher Martin. "He's got arms the size of my thighs."

"Very impressive," said Dacre AJ. "I must remember to never upset him!"

Later that evening in the canteen, whilst on their second pint, Shepherd Neame bitter, the little group of pioneers were explaining the trials and tribulations of having been film stars, well not quite stars, more like extras. The previous summer had seen most of the trained soldiers and a good number of the recruits involved in the making of the film *The Longest Day*.

As Timber Woods explained, "We had to do our beach landing several times because the actors couldn't get it right. Then the American marines wouldn't do their landing, said it was too rough. So instead of delaying it for several more days, they gave us lot GI helmets and sticks of chewing gum and told us to do it – bloody cheek."

"Did you get paid?" asked Dacre AJ.

"Did we fuck! All we got was a new set of battledress and some boots," replied Timber.

"We were all sleeping in marquees behind the sand dunes on Gold Beach. It was good fun when the actors came around for a beer or two, especially as they were paying," said Taylor. "When you see the film, watch out for Brum Preece dressed as an American. When he gets shot, he gives a little wave as he falls over, it's a real laugh."

There was a momentary lull in the conversation, then Dacre AJ said, "So tell me, what's it like being a trained soldier here at The Depot."

The others looked at each other trying to decide who should go first. Pincher Martin started, "It's okay, we keep our room marine clean, that keeps the CSM out of our hair. We've learnt not to smile back at the Company Commander."

Dacre interrupted, "What's all that about anyway?"

Fagin replied, "He got wounded in the face during the Suez bit, so he has a twitch which, to the uninitiated, looks like a smile. But God help you if you smile back!"

Martin continued, "The CO is Brigadier Ellis MC, affectionately known as *Darkie*, born in India so they say, he's a real gent."

Dacre AJ nodded his head in agreement. "Yes, I knew him back in 1942, he was my troop commander, we did Dieppe together. As you say, a real gent."

Martin paused before continuing, "The adjutant is Captain John Stirling, a Rupert if ever there was, he's mostly into horses and riding and all that. The RSM is Mr Mcfee."

"You mean Stuart Mcfee?" queried Dacre AJ.

"Yes, that's right, you know him?" asked Taylor.

"Yes, we go way back," he replied.

Taylor continued, "He's a very fair man, tough but fair, won't stand any nonsense."

Timber Woods chipped in, "The real problem is the second in command Major Blair, better known as 'Kipper'. All four marines then chorused, "Because he flaps about everywhere." They all laughed.

Pincher Martin continued, "Seriously AJ, he's a bloody problem, a real nobber. In addition to being the second in command, he is also the senior training officer. He virtually controls everything that goes on in this barracks, he has this place sown up tighter than a bugler's arse. Also he has this dog, a bloody great Alsatian, goes everywhere with him. It's so well trained he uses it to help him patrol the barracks. He goes one way and the dog goes the other. It's lethal, you can't hide away anywhere without the dog sniffing you out. One of my mates ended up pinned to a wall with the dog's nose buried in his crotch, needless to say he didn't go anywhere, well you wouldn't, would you."

Dacre AJ looked at all four of them. "Surely he can't be that bad?" he said

"He's worse," replied Fagin with a serious look on his face. "I have an oppo who was his MOA. He wears several changes of uniform a day, everything has to be perfectly clean and spotless – all bulled up. One day my oppo didn't have time to take the laces out of the major's boots to clean them, so he sacked him just like that! In addition, all the training teams are his and the First Drill is his main man, so watch out."

"He even did for Preece and Day," said Martin. "It's because of him they got DQs."

"Were they drunk?" asked Dacre AJ.

"Sure they were, well at least Brum Preece was steaming," replied Martin. "But Geordie always looked after Brum and would have got him past the guardroom and put him to bed no trouble. But Kipper Blair was doing one of his late night inspections, he's a bugger for those: caught them just outside South Barracks. Anyway, to cut a long story short, he calls out the guard and has them both arrested. Sod's law, fourteen days each! Even the guard commander and the duty sergeant were embarrassed.

"Here's another thing," said Woods, "A year ago our beloved major introduced a competition called the *Hunter Challenge*, canoeing, shooting, fitness and so on. It takes place three times a year. It's even been incorporated into the recruits training programme. His bloody team wins every sodding time!"

"It's because he has the pick of the training teams," said Fagin, "You know the PTIs and PWIs.

"Don't forget the Drill Instructors," said Taylor, "especially them."

Dacre AJ sat for a moment or two taking all of this in. " If the CO and the RSM are so good, how come they haven't done anything about this?"

"Ah ha!" said Martin, "There's the nub of the problem. I have a friend in the training office who tells me that the number of recruits is at an all-time high, consequently their lordships at the Admiralty are so impressed that The Depot must keep this going at all costs. The CO and the RSM have their hands tied behind their backs, so to speak. There's not a damn thing they can do about it, as much as they would like to I'm sure.

Much later, when the duty bugler had sounded lights out for the recruits, Dacre AJ lay on his bed and reflected on the day's events and in particular why had he been sent to The Depot and was it somehow connected to what the others had told him about the situation here in the barracks. Oh well, he thought, it was no use worrying over things that you have no control over, that was what his grandfather had taught him. Perhaps all would be revealed when he saw the Commanding Officer in the morning.

# 4

MOST of the good citizens of Walmer and Deal were sound asleep in their warm beds. It was 0558 hours and it was still dark. The duty bugler left the guardroom and marched briskly along the road towards the parade ground, the heels of his boots striking rhythmically on the tarmac, the sound echoing off the walls of the nearby buildings. He halted in front of the flagpole, turned smartly to his right, wet his lips with spit and brought his bugle to the play position.

Dacre AJ awoke immediately as the first note of reveille sounded. As he checked his watch, the others in the room began to stir and bedside lights were switched on as the marines began to get up. Within five minutes everyone was up and busy, dressed for the most part in shorts and flip-flops. Each one of the group cleaned his allocated part of the room: windows, ledges, table, chairs, spittoon, beds and lockers. If it stood still, it got cleaned and polished, nothing was missed. Dacre AJ was impressed. This was very well organised, particularly since two of the room were missing.

"It's the Company Commander's rounds this morning so we need to look good," explained Pincher Martin.

"Anything I can do to help?" asked Dacre AJ.

"Nope, it's all covered, thanks. Do your own bed space and perhaps have a look to see if we have missed anything, that would be a help," replied Martin. Thirty minutes later all was finished; the floor had even received a coat of polish, ready to be buffed up after breakfast.

"Well, what do you think?" said Fagin.

Dacre AJ looked around the room. "Good! In fact very good," he said slowly.

"Have we missed anything?" asked Taylor quietly.

"Are you serious?" he replied.

"Of course we are, have we missed any fucking thing or what?" said Martin aggressively.

Silently, Dacre AJ reached into his cupboard drawer and took out an old pair of white gloves. Putting on the right hand glove he walked across to one of the spare beds. Lifting the bed-end he ran his gloved hand underneath the leg of the bed. It was dirty. Someone quietly said an expletive. Five minutes later all beds were immaculately clean.

"Thanks AJ," said Martin somewhat begrudgingly. "Now let's get some breakfast."


Dacre AJ was alone in the room, the other marines had already turned to, since they needed to be out of site of the parade ground before the 'fall-in' was sounded.

As Pincher Martin explained, "Today is the First Drills parade and, since he doesn't like us pioneers, we keep well out of his way." The deck of the room was so superbly polished you could actually see your face in it. On his way out Martin called out," AJ, watch your hob-nails on the floor when you leave, will you, it would be appreciated." Dacre AJ waved a reply.

He began to dress. As he did so, he heard the bugler on the parade ground sound the fall-in. From his window he had a grand stand view of what was going on. He counted as many as ten different squads lining up at the edge of the parade ground down by the very high wall; he estimated maybe over three hundred men. Most of the squads were in battledress with their highly polished black belts and gaiters, several squads were in fighting order and one squad was in best blues and greatcoats. The whole of the parade ground had gone very quiet. There was an air of expectancy as the First Drill marched to his position in front of the dais. Dressed immaculately in his best uniform, with his black pace stick under his arm, he appeared to be the very personification of the perfect drill instructor.

"Paaraade!" His voice carried effortlessly to all corners of the parade ground; everyone, recruits and squad instructors alike, braced themselves. "Markers faaall in!" Immediately, the right hand man of each squad sprang to attention, then marched the regulation thirty paces and halted. Whether by luck or judgment, this was perfectly timed; the markers took up their dressing from the right hand man. The First Drill cast his expert eye approvingly over the markers; that was well done, he thought. He took a very deep breath right down into his stomach, "The parade will advance. Quiiick march!" Every man on the parade ground sprang to attention, counted the correct pause and stepped off. The squad instructors were shouting out the time, left, right, left, right, as each body of men moved to their respective marker. The tramp of boots, heels first striking the ground in perfect unison, echoed off the walls of the buildings that surrounded the parade ground.

Dacre AJ turned away and closed his window. He had to admit it was an impressive performance. The Corps, his Corps, was in good hands if these youngsters were anything to go by. He took a last look around the room just to make sure that everything was squared away, then made his way downstairs and across to the guardroom and the main gate. He felt good and knew he was well turned out. He paused in front of the full length mirror fixed to the outside wall for a final check. The sign above said, '*Going ashore be smart.*'

A couple of recruits came out from the guardroom, they looked at him with something akin to awe, envy certainly; the green beret, the commando flashes, the crimson and gold unit lanyard, his medal ribbons, his King's badge and his three long service stripes, thinking perhaps of the day when they might number amongst the armed forces elite. The Regimental Policeman on gate duty gave him a nod and smile with a cheerful "Morning Badge," as he passed by. Dacre AJ marched smartly across the road that divided the two barracks and entered the gates to South Barracks, which had formerly been a cavalry barracks prior to the Royal Marines turning it into their training depot. On the way he noticed how low the sun was in the sky and that the pavements were still moist from the overnight dew. Sea gulls wheeled overhead and screeched. He could even taste the salt in the air.

Having dropped off his pay book at the Imprest Office, he made his way to the Orderly Room. The sergeant in charge who was checking names on a clipboard looked up as

Dacre AJ entered.

"Ah! You must be Marine Dacre from 43 Commando RM. You're the last one to see the Commanding Officer this morning, so wait over there." He pointed to the back of the room. The sergeant looked around. "Defaulters first, then request men, then new arrivals, got it? When it's your turn the RSM will march you in!" With that he made his way back to his desk and a mound of paperwork. Dacre AJ looked around. This was a typical OR. Every wall had a noticeboard and all the notices were squared up. The floor was well polished, although much of it was covered with coconut matting, nothing was out of place, everything marine clean. A door in the far wall led to the CO's office. Looking at the width of the main door, he presumed that in an earlier life these offices had once been stables. There were three others due to see the CO that morning. He looked at the defaulter, a young recruit, maybe sixteen or seventeen years old, seated on a chair, his right hand heavily bandaged. He was flanked by two huge Regimental Policemen. The fact that they were in best blues and he was in fatigues seemed to add more pathos to his situation. The recruit looked miserable, hurt, even frightened. He had clearly been crying. One of the policeman caught Dacre AJ's eye, who he recognised from the previous day and nodded towards the youngster. Moving across the room the policeman spoke out of the corner of his mouth.

"He's been a daft bugger. Tried to work his ticket out of the corps by cutting off his trigger finger, used his clasp knife and got one of his mates to drop a bed end on it. Sod's law though, it all went wrong and took off the tops of all four fingers! So now he's going outside, discharged unsuitable. And do you know what, this'll make you smile, he now realises he doesn't want to go. Stupid bugger!"

Dacre AJ looked at the young lad. Was basic training that bad, he wondered? He couldn't remember, his was so long ago. The old adage came to mind, *'If you can't take a joke you shouldn't have joined up,'* but perhaps that was being a bit unfair.

The policeman nodded towards the other two marines, one was a corporal, the other a sergeant. "They are both going outside, into the removal business so I hear, been moonlighting for over a year now. Good luck to them I say and roll on my time!"

The orderly room sergeant looked up from his desk towards the wall clock; it was one minute to ten. "Get ready!" he said. The two policemen took their places fore and aft of the prisoner. All stood to attention, expectantly. The CO's door opened, the RSM appeared briefly in the doorway and then in a staccato-like voice, "Prisoner and escort quiiick march, left, right, left, right, right wheel, halt! Left turn! Do not salute!" The door closed. Ten minutes later, the CO's door opened and the prisoner and escort marched out in quick time, back to the sick-bay where the recruit was to complete his discharge routine. As the corporal and sergeant took their turn, Dacre AJ wondered again what he was he had been sent to The Depot.

# 5

THE Commanding Officer's door opened and Dacre AJ marched in to the commands of the RSM. He halted in front of a large desk and looking straight ahead snapped up a smart salute. The CO looked up from the papers on his desk. The RSM barked out,

"Chatham X 06821 Marine Dacre AJ, recently arrived from 43 Commando RM, Plymouth, Sir!"

The CO took a long hard look at the marine standing in front of him. "Stand at ease Dacre; it's been a long time, hasn't it? Why, it must be nearly twenty years since we last met."

Dacre AJ reflected that, although the Corps was quite small, maybe twelve thousand men in total, it wasn't that unusual for paths not to cross, such was the complexity of how the marines were organised and drafted. He made eye contact for the first time. "Yes Sir!"

"I expect your wondering why you are here and not on your way to Aden with 43 Commando," said the CO.

"Yes Sir, something like that." He looked carefully at the man seated in front of him. He hadn't changed that much: now in his mid-forties, greying hair at the temples, a well-trimmed moustache, his dark skin, the red tabs on his battledress lapels, and the three rows of medal ribbons. This was an experienced officer, one who had seen and done much, yet would make light of it. The office was quite impersonal, a picture of Her Majesty the Queen on one wall and on the other that of the Captain General of the Royal Marines, HRH Prince Philip. On the desk a name board, *Brigadier Graham Ellis MC RM*.

On either side a paperweight, one from the USMC, the other from the Royal Dutch Marines. Dacre AJ refocused on what the CO was saying.

"...and so I need some help and I am advised that you are the man to do it. I have read your R141, and I have to say you have all the experience that I am looking for. Despite the fact that you have always turned down promotion, you are nevertheless highly thought of in the Corps. In fact, I would go so far as to say you are somewhat unique, I don't know of any other King's badge holder who has chosen to stay in the ranks. Do you, RSM?"

"No Sir, as you say, quite unique!"

The CO looked at his RSM for a brief moment. Did he detect something in that reply? Perhaps not. Dacre AJ wondered where this was all going.

The CO lowered his voice slightly, as if someone else might be listening in to their conversation. "Look Badge, I won't beat about the bush, I want you to take over the Pioneer Section and to train them up for the next Hunter Challenge Cup competition. These marines are basically good men who have just lost their way a bit. They have all failed at something or other and now the Corps is failing them. I don't like to see good men going to waste. I want you to give them back some pride and a sense of purpose. Are you agreeable to this?"

Dacre AJ quickly realised that he was expected to give an answer and since he couldn't think of a reason why not, he agreed.

"Good!" said the CO. "The RSM here will give you further details and answer any questions you might have."

The RSM responded automatically. "Attention! Salute, right turn, march out! Report to my office immediately!"

Brigadier Ellis turned to his RSM. "Well, Mr McFee, what do you think, will he do?"

The RSM paused before answering, "He'll do just fine Sir. I can't think of a better person for the job."

"Good! Give him a full briefing and let him know what he is up against and what we expect of him. Give him all the help you can, but make sure he understands that he will have to find his way in most things. Thank you, Mr McFee, that will be all for the moment. Keep me informed of progress and let us hope this is going to work."

"Sir!"

As soon as the RSM had left, the Brigadier flicked on his intercom switch. "Petty Officer Kelly, step into my office for a moment please." There was a knock at the door and a Mawrn PO entered. Tall and slim with red hair, she was wearing a dark blue serge uniform with blue badges of rank on her arm. He looked up and smiled. Since the death of his wife three years ago in a car crash, he had had little love interest in his life. Petty Officer Susan Kelly, or Sue to her friends, was a lovely young woman with everything in the right place and more. But for some reason or other he had held back from an involvement. Why? He couldn't put his finger on it, but there was he felt something perhaps not quite right.

"Ah Sue, I want you to put a call through to the Commanding Officer of 43 Commando at Stonehouse Barracks in Plymouth. Oh and Sue be discreet please."

""Yes Sir, right away."

Whilst waiting, the Brigadier took the opportunity to re-read the marine's personal file. Whilst his service record read like a boy's own adventure story, action here and medals there, in almost every theatre of war imaginable; it was the personal details that made the most fascinating reading and, in particular, gave some indication as to the character of this most unusual marine.

*<u>Father:</u> Barton J Dacre, Born: 1892 Sydney – orphan. Australian Diplomatic Service. Married 1920. Died 1921, climbing accident Dolomites, Italy; 8 months before his son was born.*

*<u>Mother:</u> Maria Maculata (nee Manzioni) Italian. Born 1901, Ravello, Italy. Married 1920, died 1921 in childbirth.*

*Brought up by his grandfather Panteleone Manzioni, businessman, successful importer of olive oil and fine Italian wines. (Panteleone's wife died 1918, Flu epidemic.)*

*Was left a small legacy and a house in Tankerton Kent by his grandfather, died 1939 London.*

*<u>Education</u>: attended a minor public school until aged 17 years. Has a natural flair for languages, fluent in French, Italian and Spanish with passable German. Over the years has acquired a working knowledge of Cantonese, Korean and Malay. Excelled in navigation and map reading. As a teenager learnt to ski and*

*climb near the family in Ravello. Also an expert canoeist and sailor.*

<u>*Marital Status*</u>*: Unmarried, his fiancée was killed at the Hendon Air Show disaster in 1948.*

The phone on his desk rang. "You are through Sir."

"Mark? Good morning, Graham here, how are you?"

"Fine thanks. You caught me just in time. I'm off to join my unit on HMS Albion, we're bound for Aden, linking up with 40 and 45 Commando. Has he arrived?"

"Yes, all safe and sound. I have just seen him. He'll do the job I think, just what we need. So many thanks, I owe you one."

"You certainly do, but anything for an old friend."

"Are Liz and the girls well?"

"Yes thanks, all fine."

"Good! Okay, I'll let you get on, have fun in the desert, goodbye for now." With that the Brigadier hung up. He hoped he had got this right. Was Dacre really the right man for the job; it was all a bit of a gamble really.


Dacre AJ knocked on the door marked *Regimental Sergeant Major* and entered. The RSM got up out of his chair from behind a very large glass-topped desk, a broad and genuine smile on his face. "AJ you old bugger, it's good to see you!"

They shook hands, firm in a long friendship that went back to their recruit training days when as squad mates they had been competing for the coveted King's Badge.

"Jock, you don't look a day over forty and that marine haircut doesn't disguise it one bit."

"How come you look ten years younger than me?" replied the RSM.

The marine looked around the neat and well-ordered office. "Well, apart from clean living I don't have any of this to contend with."

"No, that's true." The RSM looked at his old friend steadily, his smile replaced by a slight frown. "You know AJ, you must be the most decorated marine in the Corps. You've seen action all over the world, and yet you still insist on carrying those three long service stripes. I never did understand why."

Dacre AJ looked kindly at his old friend. "No, well, I wouldn't expect you to understand, but it has always been my choice."

The RSM shrugged. He flipped a switch on his phone. "Sue, could you rustle up two mugs of your best tea, please.?"

"Aye, aye Sir!" came a crisp reply.

"Sit down AJ, we need to talk."

The door opened and the tall good-looking PO Mawrn came in with two mugs of tea. She smiled warmly at the RSM and gave a small sideways look at the marine, with just a hint of admiration. The RSM nodded his head in thanks as she left. When the office door closed, he reached down into a bottom drawer of his desk and pulled out a bottle of pusser's rum. He poured a large tot into each mug. Dacre AJ raised an eyebrow inquisitively.

"I know the Master-at-Arms on HMS Bulwark," was all the RSM said. "Cheers!"

Both men took a long pull of their tea. The marine was the first to break the silence.

"So what gives? I haven't been brought up here just to beef up some tired old pioneer section, even if they are good lads. There must be more to it." The RSM took another long pull on his tea before answering.

"Yes, you are right, there is more to it, but it is tricky, so it will need careful handling."

For the next thirty minutes or so the RSM spelt out the situation regarding the second in command, Major Blair, much as the pioneers had told Dacre AJ the night before. The RSM summed it all up.

"This whole challenge thing has got out of hand, it's become too competitive. Whilst there is no doubt it has helped the training programme, it is causing us some serious problems. Not only has Major Blair handpicked his team, and consequently never loses, it is how he does it, that is our real problem. His team are all young keen JNCO's. He has promised each of them that he will get them all on the next senior promotion course down at Lympstone, but is actually holding back their applications. As a result of this, plus how the recruiting figures are seen at the Admiralty, he is cock-a-hoop."

Dacre AJ thought about this for a moment or two.

"So you and the CO want me to knock him off his perch, so to speak, by using the pioneers?"

"That's the general idea, but the CO wants it done discreetly." The marine made a sucking sound as he drew in a very long breath.

"How long have I got?"

"The next challenge is due to take place in about six weeks time. I want you to talk to the section tonight and if they go for it, put together a training programme. If there are any problems, then come to me direct. I'll help where I can, but you will need to scrounge equipment and the rest as best you can. Are there any problems that you can see?"

Dacre AJ thought for a moment or two. "Two of the pioneers are in DQs. I understand the second in command caused them to be there. I think it would help if they were part of this." The RSM nodded.

"I'll speak to the Provost Sergeant and then square it with the CO later. You can collect them at 2100 hours after the Orderly Officer has done his rounds. Anything else?"

"When we have finished this challenge, Major Blair will be gunning for these lads and I suspect he'll make their lives a misery. It might be a good idea if they could be posted somewhere else. It doesn't matter to me since my time in the Corps is nearly up. But some of these blokes have still got some service to go."

"That's a tall order, but I'll see what I can do. Let me have their preferences tomorrow when you bring over the training programme. But no promises mind, make sure they understand that! The CO will keep his distance from all this for obvious reasons, but he will be keen to know how things are going," The RSM paused, "You and he go back a bit do you?"

Dacre AJ smiled. "Yes! A long way back. Dieppe 1942. He was my Platoon Commander. We actually assembled here at The Depot, mostly volunteers from the RM Division, and were formed into the new Royal Marines 'A' Commando. We trained up in Scotland at Glen Borrowdale and Acknacary, then later on the Isle of Wight. At Dieppe we were going ashore on White Beach from a landing craft when I got shot in the arm and fell into the sea. Despite orders not to stop for anyone, he jumped in and dragged me to safety. So I guess I owe him one. What a bloody mess that ended up, the biggest cock-up since the Somme; it was like a sea version of the Charge of the Light Brigade."

There was a moment's silence, both men lost in memories of yester-year.

The RSM continued, "You'll need a base, the pioneer store is a bit too public. Over in East Barracks there is a spare office above the tailor's shop. You can use that. It's out of the way and you shouldn't be disturbed except by the musicians and drummers training. See my Mawrn on the way out, she'll let you have a resume of the Pioneer Section's R141s. I've added a few comments of my own on some of their unofficial abilities. It may help. Okay AJ, that's all for now. Watch out for yourself with the second in command. He's a sod, but a clever sod, so be careful!"

Dacre AJ stood up smartly to attention, all signs of informality now gone. "Sir!"

"Carry on Trained Soldier, that's all!"

# 6

OUTSIDE the RSM's office Dacre AJ paused to adjust his green beret. Passing the Orderly Room on his way out, he hadn't noticed that the door to the second in command's office was slightly ajar. He had just gone a couple of steps past when a sharp and fairly high pitched voice called out, "Trained Soldier report to me now!"

Dacre AJ did a sharp about turn, knocked on the door and entered.

"Shut the door!" It was a command, not a request. He did as ordered, then halted in front of the officer's desk, stood smartly to attention and saluted, longest way up and shortest way down.

A very large and unfriendly looking black Alsatian dog lay on the polished lino floor beside the desk. The dog raised its head, the ears were immediately upright, sharp and pointed, quivering like a pair of antennae. It looked the marine up and down as if deciding which part to bite first. Then it suddenly yawned, revealing an amazing set of very sharp teeth; then very slowly, settled its head back down onto the front paws, closed its eyes and promptly fell asleep. Dacre AJ breathed out slowly to release the tension in his muscles; dogs were not his favourite animals.

Major Alex Blair RM looked up slowly from the file he had been reading. Dacre AJ looked straight ahead, focussing on a trophy shield that stood on the mantelpiece above the fireplace, in which the grate was empty.

"Well mister, what do we have here?" The marine remained perfectly still, Clearly he was not required to answer. "So we have a real commando amongst us, and not any old khaki marine, no gash hand eh, but one with a long and distinguished career!" This was said dripping with sarcasm.

For the first time Dacre AJ looked at the officer. He was a small nondescript man, thin with an extremely pale complexion, a narrow gaunt looking face with a small toothbrush type moustache. His straggly dark hair was combed over in an attempt to disguise the encroaching baldness. There was not a single splash of colour on his uniform, not even a single medal ribbon; a cloth carrier!

The second in command had left his chair and now stood alongside the marine, his face no more than a few inches away. "So many medals, so well thought of, yet still only a marine and you with a King's Badge. Now I wonder what lies behind that, don't like responsibility eh! Or something else?"

Spittle was beginning to gather at the corners of the officer's mouth. Dacre AJ realised two things: firstly the major was actually enjoying himself and secondly the file that the major had in his hand was actually his own service file. He wondered how the hell that had happened!

The major took a step backwards and looked the marine up and down. "My, my, you have been a busy little marine, haven't you. Dunkirk, even though you were under age, Dieppe, Normandy, Korea, Suez and the Far East. And a swimmer canoeist to boot. Well, well! And now you are here at The Depot, my domain!" The major's voice softened somewhat as he continued in almost a conspiratorial whisper. "Look Badge, I know you are here for your release at the end of your twenty-two years of service. But you still have a couple of months to go. So why don't you come and work for me, join my training team. I could make good use of your skills and experience!"

Dacre AJ was completely taken aback by this sudden change in attitude and for the moment was at a loss as to what to say.

The major continued, "What do you say Badge, eh? Nice little number for you. Well?"

The marine paused for a second or two just to get his thoughts together. "Sorry sir, but I have a job."

"Oh yes! And what is so important that you can't come and work for me?"

"The Brigadier has me to take over the Pioneer Section."

The major forced a laugh. "That bunch of no-hopers, the Corps' rubbish! Not a chance! Not even you can do anything with that lot, let alone turn them back into real marines, they are just a waste of space!"

Dacre AJ remained silent, looking straight ahead. The major had gone very red in the face and was clearly angry.

"So be it, if that's the way you want it. Don't ever say you weren't given a chance." He turned away. "Take your beret off!"

"Sir?"

"Don't you sir me, mister. Just do as you're damn well told!" This was said with almost a snarl. The marine stood easy and removed his beret and handed it over. Major Blair looked at the well-polished brass badge, he turned the hat over and looked inside, the shining brass pin gleamed in the light. "Your cap badge is brass, it should be stay-bright. Get it changed immediately, you are out of uniform!"

"Sir?"

"You heard me! Damn your insolence. I shan't forget this!"

Dacre AJ put his beret back on and stood to attention. He was very tempted to reply but thought better of it. He knew he had been insolent and deliberately so, but there was no point in giving the major a further excuse. He saluted and left the room.


Major Alex Blair sat quietly at his desk pondering the last five minutes. The interview had not gone as he had expected. Was he missing something here? He needed to know more, but what? The major felt a moment of frustration, or was it anxiety, he was certainly tense. He needed a distraction, if only momentary, risky he knew especially in the middle of the morning, but what the hell! He reached across his desk to the intercom.

"Petty Officer Kelly step into my office, will you, and bring file 69 with you."

There was a slight pause at the end of the line, as if the order was being considered.

"Yes sir, file 69 right away."

Leaving her office PO Susan Kelly wondered how her relationship with Major Blair had come to this. She didn't love the major and wasn't even sure she really liked him. Truth be told there was something almost cruel about him. His moods could change instantly, one minute he was charming, even gallant, and the next he was vicious and hurtful. She had learnt to her cost that he never forgave a slight. They had met at an officer's mess dinner almost a year ago. He had just arrived at The Depot from

Portsmouth, having spent two years circumnavigating the globe on one of Her Majesty's ships. She was on the rebound from a long-term love affair that had just ended. They had fallen into a relationship where sex had become the driving force, anytime, any place, anywhere. True, the sex was good, well actually more than good, even if a bit rough at times. But she thought there must be more to life than this. She wondered about the marine she had seen that morning in the RSM's office, perhaps he would be different from all the others, but then again perhaps not! Two minutes later she entered the major's office, quietly closing and locking the door behind her. The dog looked up at her as she entered the room, it recognised her perfume from her many other visits and went promptly went back to sleep, it was used to this. As she crossed the room Susan was already removing her navy jacket and black tie and was beginning to undo the buttons of her crisp white blouse. The major watched her, a slight smile playing around the corners of his mouth. As he moved to the windows to close the blinds, she was already stepping out of her skirt.

"Well now my little sailor, what shall it be today?" the major said.

# 7

DACRE AJ made his way along the gravel drive to East Barracks. He had decided to check out the office that the RSM had said was available to him and anyway he needed somewhere quiet to think and plan. On his way across, he thought through the two interviews that he had had that morning. The CO and the RSM were fairly straightforward, given that they had their own agenda, and that he was the important cog in their wheel. However, the Major was something else. Clearly unpredictable and maybe, just maybe a little unstable. His vindictive comment about 'khaki marines,' that was those who chose to serve in the commando units rather than at sea might offer a clue. He knew that for some officers and, indeed some men in the ranks, real marines went to sea. Dacre AJ recalled visiting the barracks at Eastney in Portsmouth in the early 1950s, the *Alma Mater* of naval gunnery for Royal Marines since the days of the old 'blue marines', and the spiritual home of seagoing marines. At that time he had been wearing his commando flashes and a green beret and had received some very odd looks and even some hostile glares from other marines who wore the marine blue beret with its distinctive red patch behind the cap badge. In those days a marine only wore his green beret when in a commando unit. At all other times the blue beret took precedence. Consequently, for a time the Corps had been divided into 'them and us'. The sea-service marines felt that the Corps real job was on board ships as opposed to being in the commandos. Thankfully, much of that attitude had died out by 1960, although he could recall a story of a fairly senior officer commenting that he hadn't joined the Royal Marines to play soldiers. Perhaps the major had really been a ship's marine, never happier than when he had been commanding his own detachment on a cruiser or even an aircraft carrier, master of his own little empire so to speak. Of course there was little call these days for majors to command detachments, especially as the big ships began to disappear from the Royal Navy's order of battle. Perhaps that was how the major had ended up at The Depot. The RSM had been right, he would have to be careful, the second in command was clearly not an officer to antagonise. What concerned Dacre AJ was that he had probably already done this.

He found the office without any trouble. It was above the tailor's shop as the RSM had said. It was accessed by a dark flight of stone steps that had been worn down over the years by countless pairs of hobnailed boots. The noise from the practising musicians and drummers who were using the rest of the building was incredibly loud, Consequently, the office was anything but quiet. The room had clearly not been used for some time, it was dusty and dirty, with cobwebs hanging everywhere, giving the room an air of mournful neglect. The windows were so filthy you could hardly see out. The furniture was old but functional; two metal cupboards with brand new padlocks, a desk with an even older Remington typewriter, but clean and in working order, a desk lamp and a chair. In the centre of the room stood a large table and six chairs. In the corner there was a small side table on which there was a battered electric kettle, a box of loose tea, some sugar and several tins of condensed milk. Someone had been busy, very busy indeed. He didn't like to be taken for granted, but that someone had known he would take this assignment.

Dacre AJ took off his white belt and jacket and made himself comfortable at the desk. He checked the drawers: writing paper, carbon, pencils and biros, some A4 files and several clipboards. He took out a pad of paper and a couple of pencils, then opened the resumes on each of the pioneers and began reading. As he did so, he noticed that the RSM had indeed added his own comments using a heavy dark pen.

*Marine Day, Richard. Born Newcastle 1937.*

*Enlisted Portsmouth 1955. Served in 40 Commando RM, Suez & Cyprus.*

*Qualified Assault Engineer, expert in all types of explosive devices.*

*Refused to work after one of his booby traps killed a mother and two children during the EOKA crisis. Eventually granted a medical dispensation and returned to the UK.*

A good marine in a crisis, totally reliable despite losing his nerve with explosives.

*Marine Fagin, Arthur. Born Nottingham 1937.*

*Enlisted Portsmouth 1955.*

*Served in 42 Commando RM, Plymouth, Malta, Suez & Cyprus.*

*Promoted Corporal 1958. Qualified PTI 1, expert in unarmed combat, black belt in Judo.*

*Went AWOL, hospitalised his wife's boyfriend with serious injuries. Served 6 months in Military Prison and reduced to the ranks. Has two children – Rose and John.*

At his court martial he was described as a lethal weapon, should really have been kicked out of the Corps, but a good marine nevertheless and one to have on your side.

*Marine Preece, Jack. Born Birmingham 1932.*

*Enlisted Plymouth 1952.*

*Served in 41 (Independent) Commando RM, Korea, 45 Commando RM Malta, Suez & Cyprus.*

*Mentioned in Dispatches (Oak Leaf) for saving his Troop Officer's life.*

A good marine when sober, none better, but increasingly unreliable and a risk when drinking, loses complete control. His condition really needs investigating further, might be something medical.

*Marine Martin, James. Born Norwich 1936.*

*Enlisted Chatham 1956.*

*Served with 45 Commando RM, Cyprus.*

*Undertook SBS training 1958, passed out top of his course: canoeist, underwater swimmer, parachute trained, sniper and all round expert in weapons.*

*Failed his SBS psychological test, far too gung-ho/macho. Deemed unsuitable for deployment to Special Forces.*

Has a massive chip on his shoulder, feels the Corps has let him down. Has great potential and a natural ability, but has a short fuse in terms of his temper.

*Marine Taylor, Harry. Born Portsmouth 1942.*
*Enlisted Portsmouth 1958.*
*Qualified on landing craft (LC3).*
*Served on HMS Bulwark – ship's detachment.*
*Expert in all types of small boats.*
*Returned to shore duty – suffering from constant sea sickness.*

Comes from a long line of 'Royals'. Father was a ship's marine during WWII, served on HMS Ark Royal, grandfather RMA served on the Somme in WW1. Basically a good marine, has a natural ability as a scrounger.

*Marine Woods, Peter. Born Deptford, South London 1935.*
*Enlisted Chatham 1958.*
*Qualified parachutist 1957. Medical Orderly 1958.*
*Served 45 Commando RM Malta, Suez & Cyprus. Also 40 Commando RM – Recce Troop.*
*Due for discharge October 1962 having completed his nine-year engagement.*

A tough and often insubordinate marine, often spent time in DQs. Can't wait to get outside, pissed off with the Corps, not sure you can count on him.

Dacre AJ sat back and began to summarise his findings. None of these marines had been National Servicemen, they had all been volunteers which in a way was a plus. Not that he had anything against conscripts. He had served with several who had done their two years and then chosen to sign on for a further seven or more years. It was the two-year enlistment that was the problem, since the marines' intensive training lasted for at least nine months for everyone, regardless. Therein lay the problem for the national serviceman. After training, there was just over a year left for deployment. Of the six marines, five had seen active service abroad, mostly Suez and Cyprus. Not surprising really, considering that was how the Corps had been deployed during the 1950s. Marine Preece, the oldest member of the group, had like himself seen action in Korea, although they had never met, since nearly all of his time had been spent with the American Navy Seals. Taylor was the baby of the group, whilst Martin seemed to be the natural leader. Individually, they all had some interesting skills and experiences. Perhaps the CO was right, maybe they did still have something to offer the Corps and were not as washed up as the second in command seemed to think. Time would tell which of the two officers was right.

Several hours had passed. Dacre AJ paused and checked his watch, it was 1455 hrs. Another five minutes he thought and he was finished. He collected all of the papers together and attached them to one of the clipboards. In his experience no one ever questioned a person with a clipboard who looked busy. He smiled to himself, remembering a former mess mate who had spent nearly three months at Stonehouse Barracks in Plymouth with a clipboard and pencil 'checking' fire extinguishers. No one had ever questioned his unauthorised inventory check. Dacre AJ squared away the room, locked up and went down the stairs. The musicians and drummers had stopped practising earlier, so the building had an eerie silence. Leaving the barracks he turned right into North Barracks Road and walked quickly to the corner of Gladstone Street. On his right was a smart row of Edwardian semi-detached villas. On his left was the high barracks' wall. Following the wall he found what he hoped would be there, a small wicket gate set into the brickwork. It had clearly not been used for many years, but it had possibilities. Retracing his steps he entered the barracks by the sea gate, the sentry on duty nodded him through, his uniform and clipboard saw to that. Passing the detention quarters on his left and the senior officers' married quarters on his right, he made his way towards the stables and the pioneer stores which were tucked away in the far corner backing on to the barracks' wall. It was very quiet with no one about, save a groom busy in the stables expertly brushing down one of the adjutant's horses; he never even looked up as the marine walked past. The pioneer store was closed and locked up. He walked between the two buildings and then carefully picked his way through a collection of old signs, rusting wheel barrows and disused cast iron railings, most of which were overgrown with weeds and stinging nettles. Clearly an area of the barracks overlooked by everyone. In the far corner was the wicket gate, heavily barred with several very old padlocks. He grunted in satisfaction; this was looking good, he thought.

Dacre AJ made his way back towards the drill shed. He stopped just outside the glass-fronted Drill Instructors' office. On the parade ground to his front was a squad of about sixty recruits standing at attention in front of the dais. The First Drill was obviously giving them a good talking to as he was punching the air with his pace stick in order to emphasise whatever he was saying. Dacre AJ was suddenly aware of someone standing beside him. He took a quick sideways look, It was a corporal drill instructor in a uniform he didn't recognise. Both men stood silently for a moment or two, watching the recruits receive their parade ground lecture. Their silence was interrupted by the sound of a horse coming up the road behind them. Without bothering to turn around, both marines automatically stiffened their backs, since the only person with a horse was the adjutant. The corporal let out a 'oh dear lord' as a recruit leading one of the adjutant's horses ambled past them heading for the parade ground. Recovering from his surprise the corporal barked out a command, "Recruit Meacher, report to me now!" The recruit skilfully wheeled the horse in a tight circle and came to halt in front of the corporal. "What the bloody hell are you doing with Adjutant's charger?" asked the corporal.

"Well Corp…" He was immediately interrupted.

"Stop! I'm not bloody dead, am I? Not a corp or corps! I am a Corporal and don't you forget it. Start again." The recruit went red in the face with embarrassment.

"Sorry Corps, I mean Corporal. The First Drill sent me to find a horseshoe. He said that since I couldn't march for love nor money, I might as well do something useful. I couldn't find a horseshoe so I brought a horse instead. You are always telling us to use our initiative, so I did." Both Dacre AJ and the Corporal found it extremely difficult not to burst out laughing. Somehow they remained in control of themselves and managed to keep a straight face; the young recruit was clearly in earnest. With a deadly serious face, the corporal spoke slowly and quietly.

"Recruit Meacher, I want you to take this horse back to the stables and hand it over to the groom. If he is not there, then wait for him. After that you are to report to me directly. Is that clear?"

"Yes Corporal. But there is one thing."

"Yes Meacher. What?"

"The horse has a cracked shoe."

"What?"

"One of its shoes is cracked, you can hear it as the horse walks."

"Know about horses, do you Meacher?"

"Yes Corporal. I was a farrier in civvy street."

"And you joined the marines? Why not the cavalry?"

"Someone at home told me to go and join the *horse marines*."

The Corporal and Dacre AJ looked at each other in utter amazement. The Corporal let out a long and heartfelt sigh.

"Meacher, just go and wait for the groom, tell him the problem, then come back to me immediately, got it?"

With the recruit and the horse gone the corporal turned to Dacre AJ.

"He won't make it much longer, you know."

"Why?" the marine asked looking at the departing pair.

"He can't straighten his arms, something to do with the muscles. I'm not sure what. Anyway he is up for medical discharge. After all you can't have a Royal who can't march, can you?" The marine thought about this for a moment before replying.

"No, I suppose not. Seems a shame though, he is obviously good with horses."

The corporal nodded towards the parade ground. "Watch this badge, this will be good. The First Drill is supposed to be teaching them a darned good lesson."

"Why?" asked the marine.

"They are not shaping up very well, plenty of squad spirit and some good potential lads, but their basic drill is so poor, they just can't seem to get it together."

"Who are the three in navy uniforms at the back of the squad?" asked Dacre AJ.

"They're from the Royal Brunei Navy. They are doing a crash course on how to be a marine, later they will go Lympstone to do the commando course. Then they are back to Brunei to train up their own force, so I've been told. The corporal paused.

"Ah, here we go, it's the old story of the Russians are coming, what are you going to do? Some bright spark always says run." Suddenly, the entire squad broke up and ran full pelt down the parade ground to the high barracks' wall on the perimeter. Within seconds every one of the recruits was scrambling and helping each other over the wall, not one person was left.

"Well I'll be damned!" said the corporal. "No one has ever done that before. That wall must be at least fifteen feet high." Dacre AJ was impressed.

"They might not be able to march like Royals yet, but they'll make mincemeat of the commando course if they go on like that."

The First Drill stood looking at the empty parade ground in total frustration. Slowly and stiffly, he turned and marched off towards the guardroom.

Dacre AJ turned towards his companion. "What's the uniform, Corporal?"

"It's the new Lovat Green. I'm trialling it for six months. If all goes well, the entire Corps will change over in 1964, our tercentenary year. What do you think of it?"

The marine looked him up and down. It was smart, in fact very smart and well cut, an unusual colour, almost American in style, especially with the white peaked cap.

"I'm a battledress man myself, but yes it looks good. It's certainly distinctive and very different from the army's new uniform. I'm not sure about the stay bright buttons though, maybe they should be darker, perhaps like the old war time combat badges."

The corporal shook his head. "I'm not sure what their lordships at the Admiralty will say to that, but I'll pass it on, thanks. Now I suppose I had better go and help round up my squad. Knowing them as I do, they'll be all over the town taking the opportunity to enjoy themselves, especially since they haven't qualified for shore leave yet."

The marine stood and watched the drill instructor march off briskly down the road, his pace stick under his right arm. He had forgotten about the Corps Tercentenary in two years' time. Three hundred years of 'Royals', who would have thought it! He would miss all the celebrations. He shrugged his shoulders, it couldn't be helped. Time to get on; he had a lot to do.

# 8

ENTERING HQ Company building Dacre AJ stopped to check the noticeboard. The company clerk poked his head out of the office door.

"Badge, the sergeant-major is looking for you." The marine walked into the main office, knocked on the CSM's door and entered. The sergeant-major looked up from a large pile of papers.

"Ah Badge. The RSM tells me you are now in charge of the Pioneer Section, correct?"

Dacre AJ nodded in agreement. "Well, I have a little job for you and your men. Report to Band Sergeant-Major Wilson over in 'M' Company, he'll give you all the details. Go right now, he's expecting you."

Dacre AJ made his way along past the parade ground and turned right into 'M'Company office. The BCSM looked up and smiled a greeting.

"Thanks for coming straight away Badge. I need the help of you and your pioneers. As you may know our massed bands are performing at the Royal Tournament this year. In two weeks' time, over three hundred bandsmen and drummers will be descending on us from Plymouth, Portsmouth and Chatham to begin rehearsals. So what I need is for you and your team to set up an area on the playing fields over in South Barracks the exact same size as the arena at Earls Court. You can draw rope and stakes from the Quarter –Master. Here are the measurements. It's essential that you are as accurate as you can be, after all we don't want any of our lot ending up sitting in the laps of VIPs, do we?"

Leaving the office the marine made his way back up to the barrack room. The pioneers had clearly finished early that afternoon, some were cleaning kit, several had showered and were just wearing towels around their waists. There was an air of expectancy in the room. On the table was a very large cream and chocolate cake. As Dacre AJ entered the room, everyone looked up. Seeing the cake brought a smile to his face.

"Been lucky, have we?" He asked nodding towards the table. Everyone in the room suddenly went quiet. Pincher Martin immediately rolled off his bed and took an aggressive stance.

"It's not luck, as you damn well know AJ! We worked hard for that cake and we won it fair and square!" Somewhat taken aback he realised he was witnessing Martin's short fuse. Going off half-cock over a cake said much about the man and his frustrations, and indeed about the rest of the group, where winning a cake became their entire focus. Dacre AJ decided to back-track immediately. He nodded his head in agreement.

"Yeh, you are right, sorry. It's just me being a bit flippant!"

Martin somewhat pacified by the apology continued. "Anyway, we thought we would wait for you since it was your bloody bed-ends that tipped the balance, so the company scribes told me."

With that, Tubby Taylor produced a very large knife and began cutting the cake into huge chunks. Timber Woods rummaged in his locker and came out with half a bottle of rum.

"Get your mugs and plates, let's eat and splice the main brace," he said.

The cake was good, the rum was even better, a perfect way to end the day, thought Dacre AJ.


"So what's your day been like?" Martin asked, halfway through his second piece of cake. The other marines had stopped talking and were looking at AJ. Best to tell all and keep nothing back, he thought; after all he was going to need them as much as they were going to need him. So in some detail he explained his meeting with the CO and the RSM and what he, rather they were being asked to do. He also casually mentioned his meeting with the second in command, but not in any detail. When he had finished you could have heard a pin drop, each marine thinking of what might lay ahead. Pincher Martin was the first to speak.

"Well, I like the idea of a chance to stuff 'Kipper' Blair. But we could really do with Preece and Day out of DQs". Dacre AJ nodded his head in agreement.

"They'll be out this evening. I have arranged to collect them just after 2100 hrs when the Duty Officer has finished his rounds. If you all think you are up for this, I suggest we meet here at about 2115 and have a serious discussion as to how we are going to tackle this challenge." Everyone agreed.

"In the meantime I have a little job for a couple of you to do over on the playing fields."


At exactly 2100 hrs Dacre AJ rang the bell on the door of the Detention Quarters. Almost immediately, an inspection hatch slid open and a pair of eyes looked him up and down. The head turned slightly to one side.

"It's the Badge come for the two pioneers Corporal, just like the Provost Sergeant said." Two bolts were drawn and a key turned in the lock. The door swung open slowly and silently on well-oiled hinges. A marine guard, tall and solidly built waved him in.

"Report to the Duty Corporal in the office." Dacre AJ stepped inside and paused whilst the door was relocked. The smell immediately hit the back of his throat. A combination of disinfectant, paint and polish. The DQs were absolutely spotless. The walls were painted white. The deck of flagstones originally grey was almost as white as the walls, with the years of scrubbing. The fire fighting equipment, hose and extinguishers were all of highly polished brass. In the corner stood a dustbin, burnished by hundreds of detainees over the years. It gleamed brightly under the lights. In front of him was a brick-built pit, maybe three feet deep and perhaps ten feet square. It was surrounded by a double railed metal barrier also highly burnished. In the pit sat the two pioneers he had come to collect, looking very dejected. They looked up at him suspiciously as he made his way along the narrow walkway that led to the DQs office. The Duty Corporal looked him up and down, noticing his three long service stripes and his rows of medal ribbons.

"I don't know how you have managed this Badge? These two buggers have still got ten days of their sentence to do! Somebody must owe you big time. Oh well, it's nothing to do with me, the best of luck with them, you're going to need it. Sign here, here and here," he said. "They're all yours. Now get them the fuck out of my sight, they have been nothing but bloody trouble the whole time!" Dacre AJ turned and nodded to the two marines who scrambled out between the railings dragging their kit bags with them. The sentry had already opened the door and within seconds the three of them were outside breathing in the cool night air. They moved quickly and quietly past the rear of the drill shed and then along the back of the main block that formed 'R' and 'M' Company. Dacre AJ had decided that whilst it was a longer way round, it was better to keep out of site of the openness of the parade ground, there was no point in attracting unwanted attention. At that time of night the whole block was ablaze with lights. In every room, recruits, junior marines and young bandsmen were cleaning and preparing kit for the following day. The sound of music drifted across on the evening sea air. Dacre wondered how the civilians who lived nearby put up with all the noise, perhaps they had just got used to it; after all the barracks had been here a very long time. As they reached the far end of the building, Dacre AJ held up his hand to signal a halt. He signed to the others that he was going to check the way ahead. The distance between the two buildings was only about twenty yards, but it was completely open, with a clear view to the parade ground and the dining hall beyond. He knelt down before glancing around the corner. He froze for only a split second. The Duty Officer and SNCO were exercising the fire piquet on the edge of the parade ground. Fire hoses snaked from a nearby hydrant as two trained soldiers instructed a group of recruits in the finer technicalities of putting out a fire. Watching all of this was the second – in command Major Blair. Beside him was a Mawrn Petty Officer, she appeared to be taking notes. At his feet his Alsatian dog sat to attention, watching everything, missing nothing. Dacre AJ pulled back and held up his hand, fingers splayed to indicate a five-minute delay. The other two dropped their kitbags off their shoulders and leant against the wall; they were good at waiting.

Dacre AJ thought about the DQs from where he had 'rescued' Preece and Day. Every marine, trained soldier or recruit knew that the Detention Quarters was a place to be avoided. Only the real hard cases ever went back for a second time. The Depot's DQs was run as an old fashioned 'glasshouse'; it was a place of trial and terror. Everything was done at the double, the cells and the wooden beds had to be scrubbed daily. White webbing gear was blancoed and brasses polished until gleaming. Black webbing was polished until it shone, boots were spit and polished until they were like mirrors. Kit was laid out as per regulations, folded to the exact size of the marine's magazine The *Globe and Laurel*; in fact one would be used as a template. First parade would be at 0600 hrs. slopping and scrubbing out, followed by a meagre breakfast, usually cold. The forenoon would be spent on drill, in full marching order, often full of sand or house bricks and wearing greatcoats over your uniform. The drill instructors were merciless! After several hours even the fittest marine had been known to collapse from exhaustion. Back in DQs more ritualistic cleaning, polishing and bulling up of your kit. Later this would be followed by an hour or more of burnishing the dustbin. After lunch, several hours was spent with the PTIs who exercised those muscles you didn't know you had, to a point where you would be screaming in agony. Late afternoon meant more cleaning, this time the DQs themselves, floors walls, heads and fire fighting equipment. Each day repeated itself, incessantly, monotonously. The establishment tried and often succeeded in turning a poor marine into a good one. Failing that, it at least discouraged those military crimes that carried the dreaded words 'for twenty-eight days.' If your sentence was longer than that, you were either sent to the Army DQs at Colchester or to the Naval DQs at Portsmouth. Both tough places, but considered by some a holiday when compared to The Depot RM.

Dacre AJ looked at his two companions. Marine Day, the 'Geordie' stood about five foot nine, was slim but wiry. He had two long service stripes on his arm and a NGS medal ribbon, so he had seen some action. Preece, the 'Brummie', on the other hand, was much taller, broad at the shoulders, maybe six foot four and perhaps fourteen stone in weight. He was the older of the two and had several medal ribbons, including two for Korea, one with 'oak leaves', indicating that he had been mentioned in despatches.

Clearly, he had been at the sharp end at some time or other. He was also the one with the drink problem, or rather he became a problem after a couple of drinks. Dacre AJ tried to imagine Preece shaking his cell door off its hinges. It wasn't difficult to do!

He came back to reality with a start. Both marines were looking at him quizzically. He glanced around the corner again; the fire piquet was clearing up under the watchful eye of the two trained soldiers. Everyone else had gone. Without looking back, he waved the two marines forward and together they crossed the open space to the safety of their own building.

# 9

THE pioneers were seated around the table in their room; it was silent. Someone gave a small cough. Dacre AJ studied the papers in front of him, took a deep breath and began, "As most of you know, the CO and the RSM want us to take on the second –in command and his team in the next *Hunter Challenge* competition." He paused deliberately and looked around the table. "I need to know if you are all up for this. There can't be any opting out and we can't carry any dead weight. It's all or none!" There was a general buzz of agreement from around the table. He interrupted the chatter.

"No! That's not good enough. I need to hear you say yes, and so does the man next to you. This is going to be tough, so we all have to make a commitment to each other. Okay?" Dacre AJ looked at each marine in turn just to make the point. "Art, perhaps you will be kind enough to start us off. " Arthur Fagin looked around the table, he swallowed once. "I'm in, AJ!"

"Pincher, you're next." Martin looked challengingly at the marine.

"You lead, I'll follow. Yes, I am in!"

"Tubby?"

"Yes, you can count on me!"

"Timber?"

"Sounds good to me, even though I want out of this man's Corps, I'm in!"

"Geordie?"

"It's okay with me, anything to get back at that bastard 'Kipper'".

"Brum?"

"If it's okay with Geordie, it's okay with me. Let's give it a go I say."

"Good, that's what I wanted to hear. Now we have just six weeks to get fit and by that I mean commando fit, fighting fit! I want and expect one hundred and ten per cent of effort from each of you. Nothing else will do. Whatever I say, I expect to be done and no excuses, is that clear?" He paused deliberately. "Training rig will be: SV boots and puttees, fatigue trousers, shirts and Denison smocks; berets and make sure you black your cap badges with either some paint or burn on some boot polish. We will start at 0530 each morning with a little run on the beach. 0700 will be breakfast and we will turn to at 0800. We will work the forenoon on pioneer duties. The afternoon and evenings will be for training. We will go everywhere and do everything at the double! Here's an outline of our training programme for each of you for the next six weeks. Put it up in your locker and no talking to anyone about what we are doing. Brum, definitely no drinking! In fact, that goes for all of you. Keep off the beer!" There was some shuffling of feet from the group, but no one objected. Each marine was just beginning to realise what he had let himself in for.

"Arthur, you're the PTI. I want you to put together a programme of daily exercises, runs on the beach, especially the shingle, speed marches and unarmed combat, lots of it. Don't forget rope work and the assault course. I want plenty of emphasis on teamwork. You lead and we will follow. Let me have that by tomorrow morning."

"Right AJ," replied Arthur with a look of joy on his face. He was back in business.

"Pincher. I want you to look after the canoe training, so the usual form, from capsize drills to long-distance paddling. Liaise with staff at the swimming pool for us all to do survival tests, silver level will do. You and I will look after the weapons training and range work. We'll also pick up on advance techniques of stealth and assault skills. Check with range wardens down at Kingsdown, make sure we have access when we want it." Martin nodded in agreement, with something resembling a smile on his face.

"Tubby, you're the best scrounger at The Depot so I'm told. So full fighting orders for everyone and GS Bergen packs. Oh and get some house bricks, will you, a couple of dozen should do.

Liaise with Pincher about the canoes and anything else he may need. Sort out some weapons for us: SLR rifles, a couple of Bren guns and some SMGs. Oh, and you had better organise some radio training. Three R42s should do, we can always share. We'll want to spend at least a day brushing up on radio procedures."

"Okay AJ, consider it done. Although I may have some problems in getting the weapons, they are not easy to access."

"Get what you can, any problems then come to me," replied Dacre.

"Timber, I want you to get down to the sickbay and stock up with the usual bandages and plasters. Make sure you get plenty of codeine and see if you can get some morphine. Remember no one goes sick! I also want everyone to know first aid, so sort out some training, will you."

"Right AJ."

"Geordie, you're the assault engineer. I want you to get plenty of thunder flashes and smoke grenades. Also see what you can do about some ammunition for the weapons; 7.62 for the rifles and Bren guns and 9mm for the SMGs." Geordie hesitated, as if he was going to say something. Everyone was looking at him. He gritted his teeth in anguish, memories came flooding back. He gave a thumbs up sign, he could do this. Brum Preece interrupted.

"The Brens we have here are still the old point 303s. They haven't been converted like those in the commando units."

"Thanks for that, I didn't know," said AJ. "Now Brum, a job for you. Behind the pioneer store there is a small disused wicket gate. It's been boarded up and long forgotten. See if you can get it to open. It would be very useful, allowing us to come and go without attracting too much attention. But do it quietly, don't make a meal of it! Now there is something else I want you all to think about. When we have finally tweaked the second –in – command's nose, as we will, your staying on at The Depot will be difficult, to say the least. Your cards will be marked. I have asked the RSM to see if he can persuade the CO to get you a posting of your choice. Let me know where you would like to go and I will pass it on, but remember nothing is guaranteed. One last thing, we have been allocated some office space over in East Barracks, first floor above the tailor's shop. Whilst it is out of the way, it will be noisy with all the bandies practising, still it will give us some cover. We'll use it for meetings and indoor training. It needs a bloody good clean but don't clean the windows, since we don't want to advertise our presence. Brum, perhaps you and Geordie will take care of that?" Both marines chorused they would. "Finally, I want you all to remember that as I see it we are a blunt sword having its edge sharpened and we are aiming to be razor sharp."

# 10

THE young under security officer of the Indonesian Embassy in London knocked twice on the mahogany door and entered. As he crossed the room, not a sound came from his heavy brogue shoes, such was the thickness of the Persian carpet that covered the entire floor. He stopped in front of a large ornate Louis XVI desk, behind which sat the senior military attaché. He was a dark swarthy man, hairless, wearing steel-rimmed glasses, his eyes dark and piercing. A touch of Chinese here, thought the young officer.

He waited whilst the attaché finished writing, blotted his signature and put the cap back on a very expensive looking fountain pen, which he placed very carefully down on the desk. The young officer flinched ever so slightly as the attaché looked up at him, his dark eyes seemed to bore into the young man's very soul. It was well known throughout the Embassy that this man was the real authority here in London, since his brother-in-law was the President of Indonesia.

"Well, have you made the appropriate arrangements?"

"Yes sir! It has been difficult because the Irish operate as individual cells. I have made contact and arranged a meeting. If all goes well, I believe we can be successful." The attaché looked long and hard at the young man.

"I am not interested in your difficulties, only that what can be done will done and done discreetly. Is that clear? Make no mistake about this. The necessary funds have been made available to you. All the information you require is in this folder. Read and memorise the contents, then destroy it. Under no circumstance is the Ambassador or anyone else in the Embassy to know about our little arrangement. But be assured, the authorisation for this action comes from the very highest level and I mean the highest level!"

"Yes Sir!"

"I have selected you for this most vital assignment because I am advised that you are both competent and discreet. I hope that this is correct!"

"Yes Sir! Thank you Sir!"

"I am given to understand that your mother knows the President, is that true?" The young officer felt himself begin to flush, the warmth slowly spreading up his neck.

"Yes Sir!" His appointment to London had been partly achieved because of the relationship his mother had had as a sixteen-year-old with the then older congressman of the Indonesian National Assembly, who now occupied the presidential chair. In a moment of idle curiosity he had wondered if the President was actually his father, but he had never dared ask his mother. The Senior Military Attache knew all of the details already, but it amused him to see how the young man reacted. He had been correct, this youngster would do anything to protect his mother and her reputation.

"Finally, I need you to understand that if you fail me in this matter then both you and your family will feel my wrath, since I am unaccustomed to failure. Do you understand?"

"Yes Sir! I will not fail you." With that the young man turned about and left.

# 11

THE 11.25 a.m. train pulled slowly out of Charing Cross station bound for the North Kent coast. The young Indonesian security officer sat lost in thought. Making contact with the Irish Republican Army here on the mainland had proved to be extremely difficult. No one knew anything, no one wanted to talk or meet with him. But he had been persistent and this had eventually paid off. Now he was on his way to a meeting, the first of several he had been told, each one designed to ensure that he was a genuine enquiry and, more importantly, that the IRA were kept nice and safe and away from prying eyes.

He looked up as the train halted at Woolwich Dockyard, his was the next stop. Five minutes later he alighted at Woolwich Arsenal and made his way up the stairs to street level. Outside the station he turned right and walked downhill towards the market square. The street was narrow and busy; trolley buses with their overhead wires were causing some serious traffic delays. The old tram rails could still be seen set amongst cobblestones and patches of tarmac. The whole place had a certain air to it; after several minutes he realised that it must have been caused by the nearby River Thames. At the bottom of the hill he could see and smell the market place, dozens of stalls and barrows selling fruit and vegetables and others - fresh fish. The cries of the costermongers added to the general hustle and bustle of the people, mostly women and children, looking, buying, pushing and shoving. He had never seen anything quite like this before. Carefully, he picked his way through the litter of broken boxes, squashed fruit and cabbage leaves. The traffic had been stopped by a policeman to allow several barrows to be pulled across the main road from a side street. The young officer took the opportunity to cross the road himself. He was looking for an eel and pie shop, which he had been told had a large clock hanging outside. He found it easily enough. Two young boys were looking in at an open window, as a smallish man in a stripped apron was expertly catching and gutting eels. There was a long queue of people waiting to go in, some elderly, mothers with prams, even whole families. He pushed his way to the front and received some odd looks and muttered comments as he passed. It was an old style restaurant, white tiles on the walls with large mirrors. The marble-topped tables had wooden benches on either side and there was sawdust on the floor and not a spare seat to be had. Several women in green overalls were busy cleaning and wiping down tables as fast as they could. Behind the long marble counter, which ran down the left hand side of the shop, two women dressed in crisp white overalls were serving out plates of pies and mashed potatoes, then ladling on a thick green gravy. The older of the two women looked up and smiled at him, the light catching on her spectacles.

"Is Patrick Ryan here?" he asked. She pointed her spoon towards the back of the shop. He looked to where she was pointing and saw that the rear part of the shop was closed off by a wooden and glass screen; the door was labelled 'saloon'. He walked slowly to the door, pushed it open and entered. The room was completely empty except for one man sitting in the far corner, beneath the only window. The young officer slid onto the bench opposite him. The man was eating stewed eels from a large white bowl. Without looking up, he spoke with a soft Irish accent.

"Best food in the whole of London, do you want some?" The young man shook his head. "Suit yourself then!" said the Irishman. There was a prolonged silence, the Irishman continued eating. The young man coughed gently.

"I need your help!" he said.

"Why?" The young man briefly outlined his needs and how much he was prepared to pay. For the first time the Irishman looked up from his food and listened carefully, nodding his head on several occasions.

"Wait here, I've a phone call to make, I'll only be a couple of minutes." With that the Irishmen left the table and went through a door marked 'staff only.' Five minutes later he returned.

"Go back to London Bridge and then follow these instructions." With that, he pushed a small piece of paper across the table and resumed his eating. The young man sat quietly for a minute or two wondering if there was more to come. Then realising the meeting was over, he got up and left quietly. Amongst all the comings and goings in the shop no one noticed him leave.

Outside London Bridge Station the young officer took a number thirty-eight bus to the Baker's Arms at Walthamstow. Sitting upstairs at the back of the bus, he reread his instructions and having committed them to memory tore them up into tiny pieces, which he dropped on the floor. The journey passed quickly enough, taking in parts of London he had never heard of: Conobury, Kingsland, Dalton and Hackney Downs. Eventually, the bus turned into Leabridge Road. When it got to Markhouse Road, he rang the bell and got off. Remembering his instructions, he walked slowly up the road looking for a small textile factory, which was his only reference point. It was not difficult to find, its doors were open to the road, and he could see and hear the clatter of dozens of sewing machines as he passed. Passing a greengrocer's shop, he entered a tobacconist's; there were no customers in the shop. He went up to the counter.

"Five Bachelors cigarettes, please." The man behind the counter looked at him carefully.

"Sorry, we don't sell that brand in fives, why don't try these?" With that, he reached under the counter and passed over a packet of five Woodbines. The young man took the packet and left. Outside the shop he turned the packet over. There on the back was a small hand-drawn map.

Back in the shop the man reached over and pressed a small push button on the wall. Somewhere upstairs a bell faintly sounded, followed by the sound of footsteps on the stairs. A small elderly woman, her hair white and tied up in a neat bun, wearing a faded yellow nylon overall came into the rear of the shop.

"Ah, Mrs Philips! I'm sorry to disturb your lunch but I have an unexpected visitor. If you wouldn't mind watching the shop?"

"But of course Mr Gallagher, that's not a problem." Lillian Philips found nothing a problem where Mr Gallagher was concerned, for although she was Jewish and he was of the Church of Rome she had admired and loved him for many years.

The young man reached the end of the block of shops. He turned left into Avondale Road. Ten yards further on, he turned left again into a narrow service road that ran behind the shops. Walking quickly but carefully in order to avoid the numerous puddles, he found the back entrance to the shop. Opening the gate he found himself in a pocket-sized garden, complete with a small lawn and flower beds, an amazing sight given the drabness of the neighbouring properties. The back door was ajar; he pushed it open and cautiously entered. A voice called out.

"Up here!" The young man made his way up the steep stairs to a tiny landing on the first floor. "In here friend!" He entered a small dining room, the shop keeper was sitting at the table with his back to the window. There were two mugs of tea in front of him. He waved the young man to sit opposite him and pushed across a mug. The young officer sat down, picked up the mug and took a sip whilst discreetly studying the person opposite. Possibly mid-forties, hair swept back, wearing glasses, height maybe six foot or more, weight about fifteen stone, facial features difficult to tell with the light behind him. Irish certainly, but whether from the north or south he couldn't tell. The Irishman spoke slowly.

"So you are looking for some help I understand and you're willing to pay and pay well." The young officer nodded. "So then, what sort of help will you be needing?" The young man outlined his requirements adding a little more detail than before. The Irishman sat there listening and occasionally sipping his tea. When he had finished, the young man sat back and took a large mouthful of tea from his mug, it was awful. He still couldn't get used to how the English drank their tea, or in this case he supposed it was Irish tea. The Irishman looked at him steadily for several minutes as if trying to make up his mind.

"Go back to your embassy. Tonight at 8.00 p.m. be at the phone box at the end of your road. On the third ring answer it. You will have your reply!" The young officer was totally perplexed and showed it. "Ah, to be sure you didn't think we would let you get this far without knowing something about you?" The Irishman stood up, indicating that the meeting was over. The young man retraced his steps somewhat relieved and caught the next bus back to the West End.

Later that afternoon the shopkeeper made a short telephone call.

"Padraig, it's Seamus. I've met this Indonesian fellow. It's a lot of money they are offering, we could be onto something here. I think you need to see this young man for yourself!"

## 12

DACRE AJ marched purposefully towards the orderly room in South Barracks. He paused at the RSM's door, knocked and entered. The RSM looked up from his paperwork.

"Morning AJ, prompt as usual, sit yourself down." The marine handed over a buff-coloured folder.

"This is our training programme for the next six weeks, plus the list of possible postings that you asked for." The RSM opened the file and studied the contents carefully, he frowned.

"This seems a bit severe, don't you think, after all these are trained soldiers."

"No sir, not if we want them to do the job properly."

"Well okay, you're in charge. These postings? Make sure they understand I can't and won't promise! Anything else?"

"Yes sir. We need some canoes. All the ones here at The Depot are already spoken for. I thought perhaps JSWAC might be able to help us out. Ideally, I need three two-man collapsible canoes, cockles or folboats would be ideal."

"Okay, I'll see what I can do, the RSM down there owes me a favour or two. Anything else?"

"I'm going to include some rope work, free-climbing and rappelling. We'll be using the cliffs at St Margaret's Bay, it's chalk I know and not ideal, but it will have to do. Normally, we would use the traditional method to rappel, it's the tried and tested. However, our friends in the Italian Alpinare have been developing a new technique using a small metal device rather like a figure of eight. I just wondered if any of our mountain leaders might have a couple to spare, they could be very useful." The RSM made a note on a pad in front of him.

"Is that it, anything more?"

"One last thing. We can scrounge most things without too much trouble. However, weapons and ammunition are different. Perhaps if you had a quiet word with the Quartermaster, that would be a great help."

"Okay, consider it done. I'll arrange for you to collect them Wednesday forenoon. What about storage and security?"

"We'll use the office over in East Barracks. The steel lockers will be fine."

"Good! So when do you start training?"

"We've already started. Over the weekend we had a couple of runs along the beach just to get warmed up."

"How did things go?"

"They were absolutely knackered, several throwing up after the first mile or so. But no one gave up. So a promising start I think."

"Sounds good AJ. Keep me informed of progress. Once a week will do, but vary the days, it will look less obvious. Okay, carry on Badge!" Dacre AJ stood up to attention, smartly turned about and marched out, quietly closing the door behind him.

The RSM reread the contents of the file. After ten minutes he leant forward and pressed his intercom to on. "Yes Sir?" came a cheerful voice.

"Sue, will you arrange for me to see the Brigadier as soon as possible please."

"Aye, aye Sir, as soon as possible!" The RSM sat back in his seat. Things were beginning to get interesting, very interesting indeed, he mused. The intercom light winked red.

"Yes, Sue."

"The Brigadier can see you at 10.30 hours this morning, Sir."

"Thank you!"

# 13

IT was raining, that light but invasive rain, the sort that penetrates your clothing no matter how hard you try to prevent it. The street lights struggled against the gloom as the young security officer made his way to the telephone box at the end of the road. How he disliked this filthy English weather. The light from the box gave off a comforting glow. He checked his watch, one minute to go; he crossed the road and entered the phone box. At precisely 8.00 p.m. the phone rang. He counted three rings and picked up the receiver. The voice was Irish.

"Listen carefully to these instructions, write nothing down!" Two minutes later the phone went dead. The young officer felt a surge of panic, could he remember everything he had been told? Despite the rain, which by now had turned into a real downpour, he walked slowly around the entire block of buildings repeating the instructions to himself over and over again. Such was his concentration he didn't notice the rain at all.

The following day saw the young officer sitting on a tube train on the Northern Line of the London Underground heading towards the suburbs of North London. At Woodside Park Station he got off as per his instructions, and walked down the hill. In front of him on the far side of the road stood a large double fronted Victorian villa with bright yellow doors, number eighty-one. He turned right into Holden Road and walked quickly to the next intersection at Tillingham Way. There he turned left and went down the road to a bridge over a small brook. Just beyond on the left hand side was a narrow wooded footpath, which he followed until it emerged onto some playing fields. To his surprise the brook was close by on his left hand side. He scrambled down a steep bank, to where a stout plank had been placed across the water to form a crude but effective bridge. He crossed carefully, noticing that his shoes were muddy and slippery. He entered the rear garden of number eighty-one and made his way cautiously up towards the house. There were several old chicken huts, and some cold frames long disused, although one of them was full of sand and a few children's toys. Further up the garden there were rows of vegetables, some fruit canes and a small orchard. Beyond these was a large level lawn, smooth and well maintained and laid out for some game involving metal hoops. Moving furtively, he made his way to the back door, it was open. Inside it was dark with that distinct smell that suggested it was a coal cellar. He entered quietly and went up the wooden staircase which opened into a large kitchen. Opposite him was a glass-fronted dresser full of crockery and china. The room was dominated by a huge pine table and chairs, the top of which had been scrubbed white. In the right hand corner was a Rayburn stove, the heat radiating across the room. High above him, washing hung on a wooden clothes airer, some of them were for children.

"They are for my sister's children, in case you are wondering. My wife and son died in Belfast some ten years ago." There was a long pause. "Won't you sit down then?" The voice came almost from behind him and had made the young man jump. "Would you like a cup of tea?" The accent was soft Irish. The owner of the voice came into kitchen from the neighbouring scullery. He was tall, thin and wiry with thick black hair greying at the temples, aged about forty. But it was the eyes that the young man tried not to dwell on, black and devoid of any life or warmth, completely ruthless he thought. The Irishman went to the stove and expertly made a pot of tea. He poured two large mugs and indicated the milk and sugar on the table.

"Well, now my fine young friend, and what would the Indonesian Embassy be wanting with the likes of my organisation?" For the next thirty minutes or so, the young man outlined his ideas. It wasn't a plan, more a set of requirements. The planning he would leave to these experts, after all they had a well-deserved reputation. At the end of the explanation the Irishman sat quietly deep in thought, a pensive look on his face.

The minutes ticked by, the young man began to get uncomfortable, the silence was oppressive.

"So let me get this clear. You want me and my people to kidnap this man's son and to hold him for ransom. For this you will pay us £100,000, half to start with and the other half when we have finished. We are then to ransom him for a further £100,000, which when the father brings it, we may keep as long as the two of them are disposed of! Have I got that right?"

"Yes! That's correct!"

"That's a powerful lot of money, so the success of this operation must be very important to you and your superiors?" The young man nodded. "You have however got one thing wrong in your thinking. This person you want us to kidnap is not at an army barracks at Deal in Kent, if that is where he is? The nearest soldiers are at Dover and then only a small garrison. What you have at Deal is the Royal Marines training depot. You are surely not expecting us to snatch him from there, are you? Now that would be foolish!" The young man shook his head.

"No, of course not! Our information is that the father will arrange to meet his son discreetly somewhere nearby. We don't know where yet." The Irishman thought about that, but decided not to ask any questions as to how the Indonesians got their information, that was their business.

"So how long do we have to plan and prepare?"

"The father arrives in the UK early on the 23$^{rd}$ April. He will see his son that morning and then have official talks with the government in the afternoon. He should fly out later that evening. That should give you six weeks. Is that time enough?"

"It's a bit tight, but we should be able to manage to get the job done. However, you need to know that these marines are a powerful force to be reckoned with. They will not take this lightly. I know that since I have some experience of them." The youngster raised his eyebrows in a question. "Oh you needn't look so surprised. A lot of us Irish chose to fight with the British against the German Nazi's during the last war. My enemies enemy is not always my friend. My four years just happened to be with the marines, so I know what I'm talking about."

"Will it cost more?" the young man asked quietly.

"Lord no, the money is more than enough. But you must make sure that your superiors know that if and when we start this business, it could get very messy! They are tough these marines, perhaps the best trained troops in the world and I don't exaggerate. You see every marine is trained as a commando. He relies on his superior training and supreme physical fitness and endurance to take the fight to the enemy. That's why I have a lot of respect for them. It will be interesting to see how they react, even though this boyo is not really one of theirs. My thinking is that they will take this very personally."

"I see!" said the young man. The Irishman looked directly at him, his dark piercing eyes devoid of any humanity.

"Can I ask you why we don't just kill the son and get it over with?"

"It's quite straightforward really. We need the son in order to bring the father, the ransom will do that. Without the ransom the father might be persuaded not to have the meeting at all. We need to ensure that they are together, otherwise our plan will not work."

"I see! All very clever and well thought out. And just to be doubly sure, you do want them both dead!"

"Yes! That is essential to my superiors. Their future plans for the Far East depend on the deaths of these two." The Irishman went very quiet.

"That's fine then! It is better I don't know any more about your plans. I just needed to be clear in my own mind. So my young friend here is what we'll do. You go back to your Embassy and report to your superiors. I shall get in touch with some of my associates. If we decide to take this on, I shall contact you. Now, if there is nothing else, I suggest you leave the way you came."

# 14

FOR the first couple of weeks, the training programme for the small group of marines had been sheer hell. Muscles had screamed in agony, such was the punishing demands being made of their bodies. Dacre AJ was a hard taskmaster, there had been no let up! Gradually, as the men got fitter, things seemed to get better, but not easier. Even their daily run on the shingle beach, now at least five miles was undertaken with a real sense of achievement and pride, as well as a certain amount of humour. The arrival of the canoes from Poole had increased their physical capability. Their progress from the swimming pool to the sea had been impressive. Under the skilful guidance of Dacre AJ and Martin, the marines had become so much more than just competent. They could paddle for hours in all kinds of weather and not complain in the slightest. Added to this, their improved skills in shooting, rope work and unarmed combat meant that this small group of men, once considered to be less than useless, had begun to transform themselves into a serious and effective fighting force, commandoes at their very best. Both the CO and the RSM were delighted with the progress and agreed that with just a little more time, the pioneers would be more than capable of taking on the second in command's team in the coming challenge and winning!

It was a Wednesday afternoon. The Pioneer Section were down on Walmer Beach assembling their canoes for the afternoon paddle. The sun was shining and the sea was calm, small waves gently lapping against the gravel beach. The occasional passer-by walked the promenade. The still of the afternoon was suddenly interrupted by a squad of recruits, about sixty fit young men, marching along the esplanade. They were dressed in their best blue uniforms and white peaked caps. With rifles at the shoulder and their arms swinging in line with each other, their white gloves stood out against the dark blue of their serge uniforms. The crack of their boots, as the heels hit the ground in perfect unison, echoed off the shop fronts along the main road.

The pioneers stopped what they were doing to watch and admire. To a seasoned 'Royal' they were a joy to behold. The squad's drill instructor was calling out the time, left...., left...., left, right left. The recruits didn't really need this, their timing was perfect. As they marched past the pioneers, the corporal in charge nodded at them and gave a knowing wink. He suddenly gave the command to right wheel! Without the slightest hesitation, the squad wheeled right off the footpath and without breaking step, marched down onto the beach. Several passers-by had stopped to see what was happening. The pioneers stood up to get a better view as the first three men of the squad entered the sea. Those watching, stared in utter disbelieve as the entire squad was marched into the water up to their necks! The command to about turn was not given until the last three men were in the sea at waist level. Except for the passing of the odd seagull, all the watchers stood in absolute silence as the squad marched out and up the beach all still in perfect order and not one person out of step.

"Well, I'll be damned!" said Pincher Martin. "I have never seen anything like that before." The others all agreed. Dacre AJ shook his head in disbelief.

"Totally mad and utterly pointless! But such discipline. Did you notice that not one of those lads looked our way as they passed by. Absolutely insane, but bloody marvellous!"

The change in attitude and performance of the Pioneer Section around the barracks had not gone unnoticed. The Regimental Police Corporal commented as much to his Provost Sergeant one morning as they were making out the duty rota.

"Sarge! Have you noticed how that lazy bunch of pioneers are now doubling everywhere and how much time they seem to be spending on training? That 'three badger' is certainly making the buggers work!"

The Provost Sergeant had of course noticed, since nothing in the barracks escaped his eagle eye. But knowing that the RSM was taking a keen interest in them, he had wisely decided to keep his observations to himself. There was definitely something going on here, but he was he thought better off not knowing and not getting involved.

Others had also noticed this change in the pioneers. One or two of the Training Cadre had commented on it to the second in command at one of their weekly meetings. Major Blair had dismissed their comments with a casual, "It's only that old three badger trying to gee them up. It won't last!"

When the meeting had finished, the second in command took some time out to ponder on what some of his team had said about the pioneers. True he had dismissed it out of hand, yet with some further thought, there might be something going on that he had overlooked, or there was also the possibility, remote as it may seem that something was being kept from him; although what, he couldn't imagine. The more he thought about it, the more it seemed to make sense that it wouldn't do any harm to try and find out. With this in mind he telephoned the Weapon Instructors Office and spoke to one of 'his' corporals that he knew he could rely on.

"So Corporal Johns, you understand what I want you to do? Be discrete but firm. I want to know what is going on with these pioneers. Use only those men you can really trust and who you know can keep their mouths shut!"

"Yes Sir! I understand completely. You can rely on me!" Corporal William Johns, or Will to his few friends, was an ambitious young man. He had risen through the ranks quickly by sheer hard work and application. He was good at his job and he now wanted to be a sergeant. This was his next goal. Once he had achieved that, he knew that he could go all the way to the top. The major was his ticket to the next SNCOs course down at ITCRM Lympstone and he was going to be on that course come what may. Later that evening in the JNCOS Club, a small group of corporals were huddled in a corner listening intently as Will Johns outlined his proposed course of action. He had decided to go in hard and fast!

It was midday. The Pioneers had just finished their barrack duties for the forenoon. Several had already left, leaving Timber Woods and Brum Preece to do the final squaring away and to lock up. Woods was in the small yard sorting out some wheelbarrows whilst Preece was in the tiny office, on his hands and knees, picking up a collection of papers that he had accidently knocked onto the floor. The three corporals, having checked that the coast was clear, slipped unobserved into the yard. Woods turning to see if he could help the visitors, suddenly found himself seized by each arm in a vice-like grip. Johns gave a vicious punch to Wood's stomach, which drove all the air from his body. He felt his knees begin to buckle from under him and he knew he would have collapsed in agony were it not for the two that held him up. Corporal Johns leant forward and spoke in a quiet but clear voice.

"So Trained Soldier! Just what the fuck is going on with you pioneers and that old 'three badger'?" Woods was so winded that he could barely draw breath, let alone answer the question. A second crashing blow caught him unawares, this time into his right kidney. It was so painful that he almost blacked out. In the dim recesses of his mind, he realised he was in big trouble. For whatever reason, these guys meant business and he was the focus of that business.

Brum Preece got up from the floor, shuffled the papers together and pinned them onto a clipboard. He was just about to call out to his mate that he was ready to go, when he casually glanced through the little office window. He couldn't believe what he was seeing. His best oppo was being held tight by two corporals while a third was giving him a bloody good thumping. Brum moved quickly, within a split second he was in the yard. He grabbed the two men that held Timber by their collars and using all of his strength, jerked them backwards off their feet. With one swift movement, he banged their heads together with a loud crack; they sank to the ground completely dazed. Woods, finding that his arms were now free gathered what strength he had left. As the Corporal's face appeared in front of him, Woods brought his forehead down in a bone shattering head butt, smashing the corporals nose to pulp. Blood and snot flew everywhere! Corporal Johns staggered backwards, his hands up to his face. To his credit he didn't cry out, but blinded by the tears and the pain he steeped backwards, tripping over an old sign which laid him out full length on the ground with a resounding thud. He lay very still!

Preece picked his mate up from off the ground and brushed him down. Having quickly locked up, the two of them made their way back up to their room leaving the three attackers to recover in their own time. Dacre AJ was more than a little perturbed when the two lads told what had happened to them. He immediately thought of the second in command but decided to keep this to himself for the time being. Most of the others seemed to be focusing on what Timber might have done, albeit unwittingly, to have pissed off three corporals so much. Pincher Martin on the other hand looked very thoughtful. He wandered over to AJ's bed space.

"Well AJ? I smell a king-sized rat here, what do you think?"

"I think you could be right, but it would be difficult to prove. Perhaps we'll just keep this to ourselves for the time being, after all they did come off worst and Timber seems to be okay. If it is the major, then he is going to be none too pleased. Perhaps we'll get an opportunity to even things up later. In the meantime I suggest we all need to be a bit more careful."


Major Blair was not happy! Not so much because his three corporals had been injured, that was their lookout. It was because they had failed to find out anything and he wasn't used to failure. True Corporal Johns had shown a singular lack of judgement going in hard like that, although had he been successful that might have been overlooked. As it was, the major had nothing to show for the whole sorry business. The corporal stood to attention in front of the major's desk. His nose was heavily plastered and his eyes were already turning an interesting shade of purple. He looked and felt utterly miserable as the major gave him the biggest dressing down he had ever received.


The days came and went as the pioneers became fitter and fitter. They would think nothing of speed marching nine miles or more, with full kit and weapons, carrying enough bricks in their bergans to build a decent wall. Each evening was spent in their office in East Barracks studying weapon handling and the finer points of unarmed combat, how to disable and even kill your opponent by just using your bare hands. Their knowledge of emergency medical care had also improved considerably, although as one wag put it, 'we're learning how to do nasty things to people and then how to patch them up afterwards.' It was by now the fourth week and Dacre AJ was on his way to report progress to the RSM. The section was coming to the peak of their fitness and he was anxious that they should not lose the edge that had been so finely honed. These men, his pioneers, for that is how he now saw them, needed another challenge, something that would stretch them, whilst at the same time would add to their training, but what?

Brigadier Ellis sat looking at the collection of daily newspapers that were spread out on his desk. The RSM stood just behind, peering over the CO's right hand shoulder. The headlines said it all:
"BRITISH TROOPS SWEAR TOO MUCH"
"TROOPS USE THE 'F' WORD"
"Well, Mr McFee, what do you make of all this? Do we swear too much?"

"Troops do swear a lot, Sir. They always have and I suspect they always will, although I am not sure what they mean by too much."

"This paper suggests that we use the 'F' word almost every other word. Surely that can't be right, or am I just out of touch? Questions are even being asked in parliament and now this!" The Brigadier waved a signal flimsy he was holding in the air. "It's a priority order to all Commanding Officers in the UK and abroad telling us to put a stop to all this bad language and to do it immediately." The RSM was thinking rapidly about what to do.

"Well Sir, we could talk to the men but I doubt that we would be able stop it just like that."

"No, I suppose you're right. But we must show that we are at least tackling the problem. How do you suggest we handle this?"

"I suggest we keep this fairly low key, Sir. I can get all the squad instructors to speak to their squads. You could raise the matter at your officer's 'O' Group today. Then company commanders could talk to the trained soldiers tomorrow." The Brigadier sat quietly for a minute or two thinking through the RSM's suggestion.

"Very well, Mr McFee, I think that will do nicely. I'll leave the detail up to you and thank you!"

At 0800 hours the following day, Dacre AJ and his pioneers, together with the other one hundred and twenty rank and file of HQ Company found themselves seated in the Globe and Laurel Theatre. As the Company Commander Captain Dewer walked down the central aisle, the sergeant major ordered them to sit to attention. Then having reported 'all present and correct', they were told to sit at ease and smoke if they wished. The captain looked somewhat ill at ease. In all of his time in the Royal Marines he had been asked to do some strange things, but this latest order really took the biscuit. He began hesitantly:

"Men, I have gathered you here today to talk about something particularly serious. This word F, U, C, K, fuck has got stop! It is used far too often. We are receiving complaints from on high that we in Her Majesty's armed forces are nothing but a breeding ground for invective language. So I do not expect to hear any more of it. I hope I have made myself quite clear. That is all I have to say on the matter." The sergeant major called everyone to attention as the captain left the theatre, thankful to have got that over with. As the men settled back down in their seats, the sergeant major glared at them. He was clearly going to have his say.

"Now then, you fucking shower! You heard what that officer of marines said, so let that be an end to it! If not you'll have me to deal with. Is that understood?"

On their way back to the pioneer store, the marines were discussing the non-swearing directive.

"Well AJ, what do you make of all that crap?" said Pincher Martin.

"He's probably right, we do swear too much. But they'll never stop it with an order. The sergeant major got it about right, swearing has been part of service life from the year dot. We do it without thinking or reasoning, it's almost like a tradition, we all swear like troopers. Yet I wonder how many marines swear at home in front of their parents or wives and children?" Pincher thought about this for a moment or two.

"Not many I suspect. I know I don't except for the odd slip or two. I remember once being home on leave watching television with my Mum and Dad and my sister. At the end of the programme I just said 'that was a fucking good show.' I was horrified! It had just slipped out. My father who is deaf in one ear didn't hear, nor did my sister, but my mother did. She didn't say anything, I just knew she had heard me, I have never been so embarrassed."

"Do you swear when you have a run ashore?" asked AJ.

"No!" replied Pincher.

"Would you swear in front of a WRNS?"

"No!"

"Okay, would you swear in front of an officer?"

"No! Absolutely not!"

"So your point is?" said AJ.

"I don't know what my fucking point is! Just that here in barracks it's normal to swear whereas elsewhere we don't. End of fucking story!" While this brief exchange of views had been going on, Tubby Taylor had been constantly trying to interrupt them with a question. Eventually AJ asked him what he wanted.

"What does invective mean?" AJ and Pincher looked at each other, both trying not to laugh out loud, since the question had been asked in all innocence.

"I'll tell you fucking later," Pincher replied.

# 15

PADRAIG O'REAGAN sat quietly in the corner of the railway carriage holding a newspaper in front of him. He wasn't reading it, but he didn't want to be disturbed by anyone else travelling on the 9.30 a.m. train from the London St Pancras Station. This was a fast train and he would be at Nottingham Victoria within three hours, so he had plenty of time for thinking and planning. After his meeting with the young Indonesian officer, Padraig had set the wheels in motion for a possible operation. As expected, he had been summoned to appear before the Mainland Army Executive Council in order to clarify his proposed scheme. No initiative or action was ever undertaken on the mainland without their approval. He wasn't exactly nervous, more anxious that he could convince the three-man committee that this was both financially and politically worthwhile.

The train arrived on time. Padraig was met by two local Irish lads and escorted up from the platform to a large black Standard 14 saloon car, old but clearly serviceable. As he got into the back seat, he noticed that the long bonnet had been so polished over the years that the red primer paint was showing through. He didn't know why, but he found this oddly comforting. The car was driven quickly through the traffic, expertly dodging the trolley buses that crowded Parliament Street. Then down onto the London Road, following the canal until they reached Trent Bridge. Here the car turned right and in through an imposing set of wrought iron gates and onto a tree-lined embankment. The driver brought the car to a stop in front of a large and imposing Edwardian house.

"In there. They are expecting you." The driver said.

Padraig got out of the car slowly, taking his time to look around. The grass on the other side of the road slopped gently down to the river, one or two boats were moored up on the far side. This looked a nice place to live, he thought. He turned towards the house, which was easily visible over a low wooden fence. A small brass plaque by the gate said: Surgery. M Collins MD. That's clever he thought, no one would ever question why people kept coming and going. He pushed open the gate and walked up the gravel path, the garden was neat and well maintained, the lawn was immaculate. In the porch he went to press the brass bell push, when the door was opened by a young red-headed girl of about sixteen. She dropped a half curtsy.

"Good morning sir. If you'll go up the stairs to the study, the gentlemen are expecting you. It's the first door on the right."

Padraig entered a spacious and well-appointed hallway, Mintern tiles on the floor and an elegant archway. The wide stairs led up to the first floor past an attractive arts and crafts stained glass window. He knocked on the door and entered. Three men sat behind a large desk with their backs to a small bay window. A coal fire was alight in the grate so the room was exceedingly hot and stuffy. He began to sweat immediately.

"Sit down, Padraig O'Regan." The man in the middle pointed to a vacant chair. "You know who we are, so there is no need for any introductions. So tell us then what this is all about."

For the next thirty minutes or so, Padraig explained the details of the operation, leaving nothing out. It was important that these three men knew everything, so that they could make a reasoned judgement as to whether or not, he should be allowed to proceed. By the time he had finished, the room had gone very quiet, except for the tick of a clock on the mantelpiece. The man on the right leant across and whispered to the two others. The man in the middle spoke.

"Padraig, we do not normally undertake work of this sort for outsiders, let alone foreigners. Do you think this project is a good idea?"

"Since we are desperately short of funds for our forthcoming mainland offensive, yes I do! Where else will we get that sort of money from?" Silence followed his reply. The man on the left leant across to talk to the others. The man in the middle spoke again.

"Padraig. If this project is worth so much money for these two to be dead, how much more will it be worth to the father to keep them both alive? What will he pay to reverse the whole thing?"

"I have thought about that as a possibility and it would certainly increase our financial standing of that, there is doubt. However, it would mean breaking our agreement with the Indonesians. Once that became common knowledge, even in the underworld, then we as an organisation would never be trusted again! No, I don't believe that is an option for us and I therefore don't recommend it!"

The three men behind the desk went into a small huddle. The whispering was urgent and intense. After five minutes or so it stopped. The man in the middle spoke again.

"Right then Padraig, you have our approval to proceed. We shall leave everything in your capable hands. We will inform Dublin of our decision. We suggest you use Seamus Gallagher as your second in command and also as your quartermaster. Then perhaps you might use Patrick Ryan for personnel. They are both good men and well known to you. If you need any additional help, you can get in touch with our man Eammon O'Reardon here in Nottingham. Do you have any questions Padraig?" He shook his head.

"Right then! One last thing before you leave. If for any reason this operation goes wrong, we the Mainland Committee will deny all knowledge of it and any link to this organisation. We will hold you personally responsible for any of the boys who don't make it to the end. Do you understand what this means?"

Padraig looked at the three men. Deep within him he felt an anger and resentment welling up. The bastards wanted the money, but would think nothing of getting rid of him if it suited them. It was he knew a harsh regime but one he had lived with for many years. "Yes, I understand." He replied through gritted teeth.

"Okay, we're done here. Off you go, the boys will take you back to the station. Let's hope it all goes well. Good day to you now."

Much later, whilst sitting in the buffet car of the speeding train heading back to London, sipping a cup of British Rail tea, Padraig wondered about the interview. Had the committee already made their decision before his arrival? Something told him they had, but of course he would never really know. The stakes were going to be high so failure was not an option that he could even contemplate.

# 16

THERE was a gentle swell to the sea as small waves broke against the shingle beach of St Margaret's Bay in the County of Kent. The sun had begun to break through the clouds that hovered on the horizon. The Kingsdown rifle range, which had been used by the Royal Marines since 1861, lay almost at the foot of the chalk cliffs. In 1941 the RM Seige Regiment had been stationed here with their cross channel guns bombarding France. Then this part of Kent had been known as 'Hell Fire Corner' because it had been constantly under air attack by the German air force.

It had been an early start for the men of the Pioneer Section. They had already doubled down from the barracks in full fighting order, bergans and weapons to the range. Today was their final chance to test and zero in their weapons. The range was barely a hundred yards long with only six targets in the butts. One of these had been allocated to the pioneers by the range wardens, the others were to be used by a new recruit squad, their first time in the 'field'. The pioneers kept themselves to themselves, since the second in command Major Blair, was present, watching the recruits with keen interest. Thankfully, they had his full and undivided attention, due in the main to their inability to master the correct procedure for weapon handling. Despite the best efforts of the instructors, the recruits bar one or two ex-army types, continued to get it wrong. The more the sergeant shouted and cursed them, the worse they seemed to perform. Demonstration after demonstration did nothing to improve the recruits' performance. The corporal instructors were doing their best, but were fighting a losing battle. The second in command was striding up and down the firing point tut-tutting to himself, smacking his swagger cane against his leg as he walked. He looked most put out, as if something rather unpleasant was under his nose. The sergeant was deeply embarrassed by the recruits' poor performance in front of his officer; it was he felt a reflection on his own ability as an instructor. In sheer desperation, he had picked up a stout piece of drift wood and was beginning to lay about the recruits. The sound of his cudgel, for that is what it was, echoed of the cliffs as he struck the steel helmets that the recruits were wearing. Not content with that, he began striking their shoulders and backs and even their legs in his increasing temper. The marines of the Pioneer Section looked on helplessly and with mounting concern as the recruits lay in the prone position, taking their punishment without complaint. After ten minutes of this tirade, even the corporals were beginning to look uncomfortable. It was then that Major Blair stepped forward and seized the sergeant's hand in mid swing. The two men stared angrily at each other.

"Enough, Sergeant, enough!" said the major. I suggest you give this squad an hours doubling over the shingle, then run them back to barracks. That should help to teach them a lesson they won't forget."

"Yes Sir!" replied the sergeant springing to attention and snapping up a quick salute. Without another word the major got into his land-rover and drove off. The pioneers watched as the recruits struggled to their feet, bruised and battered as they were herded and prodded into three ranks.

Brum Priest turned to his companions. "You know what they say? If you can't stand the heat you should keep out of the kitchen." One or two of the others half laughed.

"There's jokes and jokes!" said Pincher Martin angrily. "What we have just witnessed here is plain old-fashioned bullying, and as far as I am concerned there's no place for that in this man's army!" Dacre smiled inwardly to himself, four weeks ago Martin would never have made a comment like that. How things had changed, how they had changed.

The recruits were by now being doubled up and down the steep shingle banks. The sun was out and what might have been described as a pleasant warm spring morning was now having a heat wave effect on the recruits. Steel helmets bounced uncomfortably on heads, sweat streamed into their eyes and rifles on slings slipped off shoulders. Some men staggered, some were carried by their comrades, only to carry someone else later, others stumbled and fell only to be dragged to their feet. It was relentless. After about an hour it finally stopped. The training corporals had managed to persuade the sergeant that some of the recruits weren't looking too good. Some of the young marines stood swaying in the cool breeze, others were kneeling being sick, their faces bright red; the steam from their bodies clearly visible, rising gently upwards. Nobody spoke. Water bottles were opened and drunk quickly to try to prevent dehydration. None of the instructors tried to stop them, even though this was not the best way to drink water. After ten minutes the squad was back on its feet ready for the run back to the barracks. Dacre caught the eye of one of the corporals in charge.

"Mind if we tag along? Some of these youngsters may have difficulty in getting back."

"Suit yourself," came a sharp reply.


Dacre turned to his team. "Okay lads, we're done here. Let's follow this lot back to The Depot, we can pick up any stragglers on the way." No one disagreed. As it turned out, the run back was pretty uneventful. One or two recruits did lag behind, clearly exhausted, yet determined not to give up. Relieved of their rifles for a while, they were soon able to catch up. One youngster, perhaps looking for a free ride back, threw himself off the road onto a nice soft patch of grass. Dacre dragged the youngster to his feet with a "nice try Royal, but it won't work," much to the horror of the three elderly ladies waiting at a nearby bus stop. Forty minutes later everyone was back in barracks safe, if not quite sound.


After a shower and change Dacre left his marines to clean weapons whilst he made his way to see the RSM for the weekly report. After talking over the morning's events with the others, he had decided not to say anything about they had witnessed. Instead, there had been complete agreement to up their training regime even further in order to ensure that the second in command and his team were thoroughly discredited.

# 17

THE tall Irishman walked slowly up the steep hill. He had caught the 4.30 p.m. train from London Charing Cross station, past Woolwich Arsenal to the next stop Plumstead.

Deep in thought he barely noticed the rows of neat Victorian terraced villas on either side of Griffin Road, so typical of this part of London. At a house almost opposite the Roman Catholic Church, he stopped and checked the road in both directions, then seeing that there was no one in sight, he pushed open the front gate and rang the doorbell.

Pat Ryan opened the door in order to let his old friend Padraig O'Regan in.

"Are we okay here?" asked Padraig. "Your neighbours?"
"Don't you worry about them. Those at number forty-eight are too old and too deaf to notice anything, whilst the woman at number fifty is at work in Woolwich at the eel and pie shop and won't be back until gone six." Padraig gave a short barking laugh.

"You and your pies, I don't know what you see in them!" Ryan shrugged his shoulders.
"It's good food and she's a good person who works hard and is left-footed just like us. Got a son who did National Service in the Guards, he was one of those that got run down by a taxi outside Buckingham Palace several years ago."

"Okay, okay! We're not here to discuss your neighbours! Is Seamus here?"

"In the back room."

"Right then, let's get on with the meeting."

The three men were seated around a small circular table that was covered in a heavy dark maroon tablecloth that reached almost to the floor; the table was set in a small bay window.

"I've been to see the Executive Committee up in Nottingham and they have given us the go-ahead for this operation. Seamus, you are to be second in command and also to act as quartermaster. Pat, you're to organise the recruiting of personnel and to take charge of the back-up team. Are you both okay with that so far?" Both men nodded in agreement.

"The situation is that we are to kidnap and hold for ransom the son of a very wealthy foreigner. For this we will be paid the sum of £100,000. We will encourage prompt payment of the ransom by sending the father a little souvenir. The father must bring the money himself, that's essential. Once he arrives, we are then to carry out our primary task, which is to kill both the father and the son. Once we have done that, we are at liberty to keep the ransom money as well. We now know that a meeting has been arranged between father and son, to take place on April 23$^{rd}$ at a place called Allington Castle, just outside Maidstone in Kent." Seamus nodded knowingly.

"I can see why we have been given the go-ahead for this, that's a powerful lot of money." Padraig continued.

"Here's how I think the plan should go. Seamus and me plus four others, dressed as military policemen will go to the castle as additional security. If we look the part, no one will question our being there. Once inside, we take control and secure the building. We hold the son, then send out the ransom demand with a very tight deadline. When the father arrives, we kill them both, take the money and leave."

"That all seems fairly straightforward," said Pat Regan. Seamus agreed.

"However," Padraig continued, "since the son is at present undergoing some sort of training with the marines, I expect they will somehow or other get involved." The other two men considered this for a moment. Seamus spoke first.

"Surely the police will handle this, it's a civilian matter. The authorities don't like the military operating on home soil." Padraig looked at both of his colleagues.

"That's the usual routine, I agree, but these marines are different. They are not your usual run-of-the-mill squaddies.

These are professional soldiers and tough, and I mean bloody tough. As I told our Indonesian friend, they will take this personally, even though he is not really one of theirs. Take it from me, they will want to be involved. So we are going to need a back-up team nearby and handy for when things start to warm up."

"Surely you mean if things start to warm up," said Pat Regan.

"No! With the marines involved it will be when! Now let's move on. Seamus as our quarter–master, this is what I want from you: firstly, a Mark II land-rover, army green with white bumpers and military police plates. Make sure the *TAC* signs are correct. Provost 28, white on black. Find out the divisional signs as well. Also make sure the number plates are army. Secondly, we will need six sets of battledress uniform with RMP flashes, also complete sets of white webbing gear, 9mm pistols, Stirling sub-machine guns with silencer and ammo. Don't forget the field caps with red cap covers and the MP armbands.

Make sure everything is clean and smart. It's important that we look the part. Have you got all that?" Seamus checked his pad that was covered in scribbled notes.

"That's fine, Padraig, you can leave it up to me."

"Now Pat, you're in charge of personnel, so here is what I want from you. I need four reliable men to be in my team. I had thought of some of the London boys, but actually if they were local lads with local knowledge, it might help. If you can find any with some military experience, so much the better. For the back-up team you'll probably have to use *sleepers* and *watchers.* Make sure the lads with me are tall and military-looking, no beards, and get them a short back and sides. The back-up team should also have four men in it. Any questions?"

"No, that's fine, I'll get onto it straight away. It may take some time, but consider it done."

"Now Seamus, we will also need a couple of safe houses and somewhere to store the land-rover. Lastly, we are going to need some portable radios, even walkie-talkies will do, a couple for each team. It's a lot to do I know, but we need this to work. Any questions?"

"Once this is all over, how are we going to leave the castle? I can't see them just letting us walk out." Padraig thought for a moment or two. In all of his thinking and planning he had not given much thought to this. Sloppy, he thought, and not like his usual methodical self; he would have to watch himself.

"I was just coming to that. We'll leave the castle on foot and walk the short distance to the river where a boat will pick us up and take us upstream to a waiting car. From there we can be away safely. Pat, you can organise that. Okay then, if there is nothing else we will meet here again in ten days' time."

# 18

DACRE stood at ease in front of the RSM's desk. He had finally decided what he wanted to do with his team of pioneers in order to challenge and stretch them even further in their training. It would mean being out of barracks for several days, and for that he would need the CO's permission. So the RSM was the best person to convince the Brigadier that what he had planned was really necessary. The RSM slowly looked the marine up and down.

"Well AJ, how's it going?"

"Fine sir, just fine. We're making good progress, the section has come on really well!" The RSM nodded.

"On the range were you this morning?"

"Yes sir, down at Kingsdown, final chance to zero in our weapons."

"All okay?" Dacre suspected he knew where this was going.

"Yes sir." The RSM stood up and went to look out of the window, a squad of recruits were marching past. Without turning around, he spoke almost to himself, "I know about the recruit squad and the sergeant's behaviour."

"Sir?"

"Their squad instructor came to see me this afternoon. He had noticed that some of his lads were carrying some heavy bruising; he thought they had been fighting. They eventually told him."

"Sir!"

"It won't do, you know. There's a difference between being tough and bullying, a fine line I know, but one we cross at our peril."

"Yes sir!"

"Were you going to tell me?"

"No sir!"

"I thought not. Sort it out in your own way, eh?"

"Yes sir, something like that." The RSM grunted.

"Okay enough of that. What can I do for you?"

"I want to take the Section out of barracks for some special training and I really need the CO's permission." The RSM picked up his pen.

"Where, when and why?"

"I want them to take part in the Devizes to Westminster canoe race. It takes place over the Easter leave period; it's about a one hundred and twenty-five mile paddle that takes about thirty hours to complete. It's physically tough and challenging and you have to dig really deep for your reserves of mental fortitude. A sort of Mount Everest for canoeists, if you know what I mean? It's just what my lads need."

"Okay, I'll speak to the CO, anything else?"

"No sir, that's all!"

"Right then, carry on."


Later that afternoon, Dacre was making his way up to his room, when the company clerk popped his head round the office door.

"Badge, the CSM wants to see you right away!" Dacre entered the office, knocked on the CSM's door and went straight in.

"Sergeant Major?"

"Ah Dacre, just the person! Got your best blue uniform with you?"

"Yes, Sergeant Major."

"Good! Get them pressed up and ready for the Zeebrugge Day Parade. Number two best dress with medals. Guest of honour will be Mr Norman Augustas Finch VC, late of the Royal Marines Artillery. You and the most junior recruit will be his escort for the day. You okay with that?"

"Yes, Sergeant Major, a pleasure!"

"Good man! One other thing, the RSM says you can take your section on the canoe trip, Devizes isn't it? Just as long as you take a couple Young Officers with you from Lympstone as a favour to their CO. It seems that one of them has shown some interest in doing the swimmer canoeist course and joining the SBS. Our Brigadier thinks you're just the person he needs to talk. Name of Ashbourne, second lieutenant, watch out for him, will you."

"Yes, Sergeant Major, and thank you!"

On his way upstairs Dacre considered these two pieces of news. Escorting Mr Finch was fine, indeed not only a real pleasure but also an honour. The 4$^{th}$ Battalion RM had lost almost half of its strength in the Zeebrugge raid in 1918. Two VCs had been awarded that day by ballot, one to Captain Bamford RM, who died in 1928 in Shanghai, the other to Sergeant Finch RMA. The sergeant had been severely wounded, but he had stayed at his gun despite the fact that all around him his companions were either dead or dying. This very gallant man had been selected to receive the Victoria Cross by the 4th Battalion RM, most of whom were RMLI.

As for taking two YOs with him on the Devizes trip, the last thing he needed was to babysit a couple of young Ruperts. However, if that was the price he had to pay, so be it! He just hoped that their fitness levels were good enough.

# 19

THE following Saturday afternoon found Dacre AJ and his team on the clifftop overlooking St Margaret's Bay. It was a dry but overcast day with a cool breeze blowing off the North Sea. Brum Priest was stripped to the waist, using a large sledgehammer to drive a couple of four-foot steel spikes into the ground. The rest of the group stood around watching and waiting, admiring Brum's effortless swing of the hammer.

"I'm glad he is on our side," commented Timber Woods to the others. Meanwhile, Dacre AJ and Pincher Martin were laying out two climbing ropes, each one long enough to reach a hundred feet or so down to the beach below. When Priest had finished, Dacre secured each rope in turn to its respective spike. Gathering the Section around him he explained that the red rope was to be used to abseil down the cliff, whilst the blue rope was to be used to climb back up. He knew it was a hell of a climb, but he had every confidence in their fitness. He then introduced the Section to the figure of eight descender, which he had managed to borrow from the Cliff Leaders down at JSWAC in Poole, Dorset. He had just finished explaining the advantages of this system over the more traditional method of rappelling, normally used by the marines, when a small group of young men, recruits judging from their haircuts, came jogging over the fields towards them. Dacre AJ recognised a couple of the youngsters from the incident down on the ranges earlier in the week. They seemed to be none the worst for the battering they took at the hands of the sergeant.

All of the recruits were wearing tracksuits and were clearly out on some sort of a recreational run. One of the group stepped forward and introduced himself as Recruit Nye. He explained that they were on their way across the clifftops towards Dover and that this was their only way of getting out of barracks for a couple of hours since they had not yet qualified for shore leave. They were hoping to get as far as the castle or at least an opportunity to explore some of the wartime bunkers said to be deep inside the white cliffs. The pioneers were full of useful advice, being somewhat sympathetic to the situation the recruits were in. Dacre AJ pointed out that the castle was probably too far to go, given the time they had available. One of the other pioneers pointed out that to the best of his knowledge none of the wartime bunkers could be accessed from the top of the cliffs; that all of the lookout posts and gun emplacements were actually on the cliff face itself. Further to that they had all been well boarded up specifically to prevent unwanted visitors from gaining access. It was at this point that Pincher Martin offered to show the recruits the way since he knew the area very well, assuming of course that he could be spared. Dacre AJ wasn't completely convinced that this was a good idea, but eventually agreed as long as Martin took a couple of spare ropes with him, just in case of emergencies. Once Martin had selected a couple of number two ropes, he led his group off at a brisk trot across the fields in the direction of Dover.

Dacre AJ and the others then turned their attention to the task in hand and spent the next couple of hours enjoying the abseiling down the hundred foot cliff face to the beach below and then cursing the hundred foot climb back up to the top of the cliff. At about 1600hrs Dacre AJ realised that his marines were tiring, each climb back up the cliff was gradually taking longer and longer. From years of experience he knew that tired men make mistakes especially when abseiling or rappelling. Indeed most accidents in mountain climbing happened on the way down rather than on the way up and he couldn't afford to have any accidents with any of his team. So they packed up their kit and, although Pincher Martin and the recruits hadn't returned, they set off to run back to barracks, more than satisfied that the afternoon had been well spent.

At about 1800hrs Martin returned. Over a large mug of tea he explained that his afternoon had gone quite well. He and his small group of recruits had managed to access an old wartime gun emplacement about twenty feet down from the cliff edge. The entrance had already been opened, perhaps by someone on a previous visit. A couple of the recruits had thought to bring pocket torches, so using these they made their way down into the pitch black interior. The steps, carved out of the chalk seemed to go down and down for ever. Eventually, deep inside the cliff they came upon a number of large chambers carved from the solid rock. Some were set up as a dining hall and galley, others an infirmary and a map room. Everywhere was covered in dust and a fine layer of white chalk; it was rather like the 'Marie Celeste', as if everyone had just walked out, albeit twenty years ago. Then they found the sleeping quarters, row upon row of bunk beds complete with mattresses and blankets. It was at this point that one of the recruits found the body. It was all wrapped up in some blankets on one of the top bunks. Checking it out, Martin reckoned the old man, possibly a tramp, had been dead for maybe five or six years. Owing to the constant cool air temperature the body had shrunk somewhat and had self-mummified. It seemed likely that the old man had forced his way in, hence the open entrance and had found his way down to the sleeping quarters. The rest was history.

The pioneers sat in absolute silence, totally amazed at Pincher Martin's exploits.

"Have you contacted the police?" asked Dacre AJ.

"Yes, I rang them from the guardroom as soon as I got in. I expect they'll want a statement some time or other," replied Pincher. "Anyway, that's not all! There's absolute mayhem in the guardroom. The Regimental Police are out in full force running around like headless chickens scouring the town for those recruits who were with me. It turns out they are over four hours adrift, having signed out for only two hours. They should have been back by 1600 not 1800hrs. There's going to be some serious bollocking going on, Major Blair will go absolutely ballistic when he finds out. So all in all a good day I think, but other than that nothing much to report!"

# 20

THE three Irishmen sat sipping their mugs of strong Irish tea, each momentarily lost in his own thoughts. Padraig Regan broke the silence.

"Right then lads, let's see what we've got, shall we? Seamus you go first."

"All of the uniforms, equipment and weapons are ready. I've tested the radios we've been given, but frankly they are unreliable. So I've gone for some walkie-talkies instead; a shorter range I know but they should do the business. We have borrowed a land-rover from our friends in the East Midlands. It's been correctly painted up and is already on its way south hidden in a removals van." Seamus then produced a town map of Maidstone and an Ordnance Survey map of that part of Kent. He continued.

"We have two safe houses arranged, one for each team. For the snatch team we have a room over a fish and chips shop, right next door to the Roman Catholic Church. It's a busy part of town so we shouldn't be noticed. It is also very close to the railway station." Seamus pointed to the town map. "The second house is just out of town, here off the Sittingbourne Road, near the old Foley House, it's on a small housing estate. It's quiet and out of the way, so we shouldn't be disturbed. The land-rover will be kept at the top of Detling Hill, here." He pointed to the position on the OS map. "It has several disused hangers and is now part of a farm. We also have two cars, not new but reliable. One will take the snatch team up to collect the land-rover. Then it will proceed down to the river and wait by these old factories, where one of the lads will have a boat waiting to pick you up. The back-up team will have the other car ready for any emergency."

"Right, that sounds fine to me Seamus, well done. Now then Pat, what have you got?"

"I've put together two teams as you asked. In the snatch team will be Joe Kilkenny, a sleeper from Maidstone who is actually a TA reservist. Then there is Liam Dolan from Whitstable, ex-national service, and Denis Haughey and Michael Hanratty both from Canterbury; these are tough men. With you and Seamus that will make your team of six. For the back-up team I've not been so lucky, good men but no military experience. I've got Donal Collins, a sleeper from Raynham, Sean Hayes, a watcher from Chatham, just out of Wormwood Scrubs by the way, did five years for his part in the Tottenham Court Road bank job. Then there is Mick Doyle from Portsmouth, who was involved in that failed raid on the commando camp down in Devon a couple of years ago." Padraig interrupted.

"These last two, since they have both got some form, have the police or Special Branch shown any interest in either of them?"

"No! We're pretty sure they haven't. In both cases these guys were just small potatoes," said Pat.

"Double-check to be sure, will you, we don't want any uninvited guests turning up to the party. That all sounds good to me, well done!" said Padraig. "Each of the two teams are to arrive individually by train or bus and are to make their way discretely to the appropriate safe house. Make sure everyone has a hot meal and no alcohol, okay? At 4.00 p.m., Pat, your car will take us up to the old airfield and drop us off, clear?" Both men nodded. "We'll have about one and a half hours to get into uniforms and to check that the vehicle looks the business. At approximately 5.30 p.m., we'll drive through the town to the castle, arriving at about 6.00 p.m. Our land-rover shouldn't attract too much attention since Maidstone is still a garrison town. We'll gain entry, secure the buildings, take the hostage and deal with any resistance, the son may well have bodyguards. Any questions so far? No! Good! At about 8.15 p.m., Pat, one of your lads will drive up to the castle. By that time we will have a little souvenir ready for delivery to the local police station. You then phone in the ransom demand and don't forget to use the current code word to show that we are a legit IRA operation and not some cranks. This should then trigger an appropriate response. The father's plane lands at Heathrow at 11.35 p.m. We'll assume the money has already been put together, so all he has to do is deliver it. By then of course the police will have closed off access to the castle, but that won't bother us. As soon as the father arrives, we take the money, complete our final task and escape by boat up the river to a point by the old paper mills, then into the car and away! Any questions so far? No! Just one last thing, should we need the back-up team, they must move quickly. Remember for this venture to be successful, it's all about timing and teamwork. Make sure that each of the men understands what is expected of them."

"Padraig, there is just one thing," said Seamus. "At our last meeting you mentioned that the marines are likely to get involved in this."

"Yes, I did. However, my most recent and reliable intelligence tells me that both commando units are occupied abroad and that the SBS and SAS are having a knees-up in Malta. So that just leaves the marines' training camp in Devon and the barracks at Portsmouth and Deal. I don't believe they will be capable of sending anyone. The army could respond, but I doubt it. I think they will pay the ransom and consider themselves lucky. We in turn must consider ourselves of the hook where the marines are concerned, I really did think they were going to be a big problem. Nevertheless, we must take nothing for granted. We need to be on our toes and alert at all times."

# 21

IT was 22.30 hrs. The men of the Pioneer Section were getting ready to turn in. There was a knock at their barrack room door. Pincher Martin rolled of his bed and stood up; he looked around the room perplexed.

"Who the hell is that?" he asked "I've never known anyone knock at our door!"

"Well, let's find out, shall we," said Dacre AJ, as he strode quickly across the room and opened the door. Standing on the threshold was the corporal squad instructor he had met several days earlier, the one with the new uniform.

"Hello Badge, sorry to trouble this late, but can I talk to you and the others?"

"You'd better come in, Corporal." By now the other marines had gathered around the table in the centre of the room. The corporal, having removed his peaked cap had sat down. Looking around the room he spoke slowly and deliberately.

"It's like this. Major Blair is very unhappy with my squad's performance, so much so that he's told me that he is going to teach them a damn good lesson. He intends a surprise night exercise for them tomorrow night, one that will either make or break them."

The marines looked at each other, one or two exchanged a knowing wink. The corporal continued.

"Just in case you are wondering, I'm not one of the major's chosen men. He's up to something and I could do with some support since I don't agree with his bullying tactics."

Dacre AJ looked around at the others, they all nodded in agreement.

"Was that your squad on the range the other morning, the ones who had the run-in with the sergeant? " he asked.

"Yes, it was. When I found out what had happened I felt I had no option but to report the whole matter to the RSM."

"Are they also the ones who went for the run to Dover?" asked Martin.

"Yes, they are!"

"Okay Corporal, we'll talk it over and I'll let you know our answer in the morning. I'm pretty sure we can do something to help. By the way, what's your name?"

"Malcolm McBride, but I answer to Jock."

"Okay Jock, thanks for coming to see us."

With the corporal gone, the room filled with an immediate clamour of talking about who would do what, where and when. Dacre AJ held up his hand for some silence.

"Okay, I gather from all of the noise that you are all up for this. As I see it, this could be an excellent opportunity for a bit of extra training, maybe even a 'night snatch'. I had thought we might take a recruit or two, or even the corporal himself. But to be honest I can't resist targeting the second in command, I think he has more than proven that he deserves this."

All of the marines broke into excited almost childlike laughter. Dacre AJ continued,

"We need to be bloody careful because after the CO he is the most senior officer here in the barracks. So this is what I suggest we do. Tubby, you and I will go out with the squad and spend the night with them. Pincher, you are to organise the others to snatch the major. I'll leave the all of the planning and organisation to you, it's better that we don't know any of the details. Just make sure that no one sees you, and I mean no –one, and that the major is back at the Officer's Mess at the latest by 0600hrs, more or less in one piece.

The following morning at breakfast, Dacre AJ spoke to the corporal and explained briefly that he and one other would be able to accompany him and his squad that night. At the last minute he decided not to say anything about their other plans, not because he didn't trust the corporal, but because there might be too many other ears that might be listening.

By 17.00hrs the Regimental Police were busy rounding up all of the members of the squad. Some had been in the canteen, a few had been in the cinema, whilst the remainder were in their barrack rooms. At precisely 17.30hrs the squad was assembled on the edge of the parade ground, wondering what on earth was going on. They were then given ten minutes to go away to get dressed in fatigues with fighting order, minus groundsheets and rifles. As the recruits began to reassemble, the major spotted Dacre and Taylor and came striding over to them.

"What the hell are you two doing here?" he demanded.

"Just a bit of extra training, sir, by invitation of the squad instructor, if that's alright with you?"

"What's in your bergans?" Dacre dropped his to the ground and opened up the top.

"Just bricks sir." He replied holding one up for inspection. The major looked non-plussed for a brief moment. Regaining his composure, he snapped out,

"Well, don't get in the way." Then as an afterthought, he added, "You can make yourselves useful by being the rear traffic guides."

At 17.45hrs the squad, led by major and the corporal doubled out of the main gates with Dacre and Taylor bringing up the rear. The major set a cracking pace as they headed out of Walmer and into the countryside.

"Say what you like about our beloved Major, but he's bloody fit," said Tubby Taylor. Dacre just nodded a reply; he was wondering how Pincher Martin and the others were getting on. With only one stop of about five minutes, he reckoned they had gone about nine miles when the major suddenly wheeled the squad into an open piece of scrub land and halted by a couple of old baths used as cattle troughs. Beside them were two empty buckets. The major picked one up and handed in to the squad instructor.

"Right then, Corporal, give me a good soaking!"

"Sir?"

"You heard me. Pour a bucket of water over me."

The corporal did as he was told and truth be told the officer stood perfectly still. Next the major soaked the corporal and then together they doused each of the recruits in turn and then both Dacre and Taylor. The major then gathered everyone around him and in a rather pompous and condescending voice spoke to the recruits.

"Now then men, you're wet, cold and tired. You have no blankets, food or tents. Tonight you will spend out here under the stars and in the morning you will present me with as many rabbits as you have been able to catch. Your corporal will make sure that there are sentries posted throughout the night. Good luck! That's all, carry on." Then taking the corporal by the arm out of earshot, he added, "I'm going for a walk down to the village. When my land-rover arrives tell him to wait for me here."

"Sir?"

"I'm going down to the local hostelry for some supper, after that I am going back to the officers' mess." The corporal stared at him in total disbelief. "Surely you didn't think I would be staying out here all night, did you? They are your squad. You can look after them and you can get your two new friends to help you out, if they can!" With that, the major walked out of the gate and headed off down the lane.


Dacre AJ and Taylor wandered over to the corporal.

"What was all that about?" Taylor asked.

"That bastard has gone down the pub and left us to babysit this lot."

Dacre looked around at the recruits, many of them were beginning to shiver.

"We need to get them organised and quickly, otherwise they will start to come apart at the seams. What do you want us to do?"

"Look, Badge, I'm a drill instructor, so I'm a bit out my depth here. Anything you suggest will be fine with me." Dacre nodded understandingly; it took a lot to admit your limitations, so he had nothing but respect for the JNCO. He asked the corporal to gather everyone around and to sit them down somewhere where it was dry. He recognised one or two of the faces looking up at him. Taking a deep breath he spoke to the silent gathering.

"Recruit Nyle, I want you and the Section Commanders to divide the squad up into groups of five or six. Collect dry sticks, then use your bayonets to cut fire pits by rolling back the turf. Use your clasp knives to pare down a twig or two for some shavings, these will light more easily. Use your mess tins and get some water on the boil. See Marine Taylor here for matches and makings, we have coffee and tinned milk. Also some bars of nutty, one between two. The heads will be over there in that far corner of the field, piss through the fence, if you need the other cut and roll back a piece of turf, then replace it when you have finished. Mark the spot with a stick so the rest of us know where to avoid. Now, sleeping arrangements. In your groups choose a good bush, clear out the underneath. Cut turfs to form a low wall, that should help keep the wind out, then cut some dry ferns for bedding. Sleep like spoons, cuddle up nice and close in order to share your body heat, and cover yourselves with your equipment. Corporal McBride will organise a rota of sentries, two on at any time. Before you turn in I want each of you to gather a couple of handfuls of twigs. You are to sleep with them like they are your best girlfriend, keep them close to you, keep them warm and dry. It might not rain tonight, but there will be almost certainly dew in the morning and damp wood doesn't light very easily. One last thing, I suspect that Major Blair thinks you are going to fail this test he has set you, so I suggest we prove him wrong by showing him just what a really good squad can do. What do you say?" One or two of the recruits smiled and nodded in agreement, several muttered "yes, Trained Soldier."

"Oh come on, you can do better than that! Let's hear you all together, one, two, three!"

With that, the entire squad with as much conviction as they could muster bellowed out, "Yes, Trained Soldier!"

Within five minutes the field was a hive of activity; fires were being lit, turfs cut and ferns were being gathered. A sense of purpose was in the air. The corporal looked on with amazement and more than a little pride.

"Well, Badge, I have to say that's pretty impressive. So, what about the rabbits that the major wants?"

"Damn, I had forgotten about those, still if the major wants rabbits, rabbits he shall have. Just let me think this through for a couple of minutes." Dacre wandered off deep in thought. He could he knew set some snares himself quite easily or he could show a couple of the recruits how to do it and then let them loose in the nearby woods. But it would be so much better if the recruits could do the whole themselves. He returned to the others.

"Okay, this is what we'll do. Get Nyle and his Section Commanders to go around and check out whether anyone has any poaching experience. If they find someone, tell him to report to me." Ten minutes later, one of the Section Commanders came back with a young recruit in tow.

"He's not a poacher, Trained Soldier, but he says he was a game keeper, will that do?" Dacre looked the youngster up and down and liked what he saw. The lad had a certain quiet confidence about him.

"Who did you work for?"

"The Duke of Devonshire, up on his estate in Derbyshire."

"What's your name?"

"Ackland, Ian Ackland, Trained Soldier," the young man replied.

"Can you snare rabbits?" Dacre asked.

"Yes, Trained Soldier."

"Good! Pick two friends and get into those woods over there and let's see what you can do by the morning." The young marine seemed to grow visibly as he blushed to the roots of his ginger hair.

"Very good, Trained Soldier." With that, he doubled away calling out to two of his friends to follow him.

As Dacre, Taylor and the Corporal were finishing off their coffee, Tubby Taylor commented, "It was a good job AJ you got me to raid the NAFFI for supplies just before we left, otherwise we would have been right up the creek without a paddle." Dacre smiled knowingly.

"That's true, but it was even better that the major didn't actually check our bergans. I guessed he wouldn't, one brick was enough to convince him. And we did need those supplies in order to give these noddies a bit of a lift."


It was almost 2230hrs by the time the major left the village pub. After a good meal of steak and kidney pudding with all the trimmings and a half decent bottle of red wine, he felt in a good mood for once. Walking down the middle of the dark lane, he was thinking about how he might creep up on the unsuspecting sentries, just to try them out so to speak. He heard an owl hoot twice. Then taken completely and suddenly by surprise, later he remembered it was just like walking into a brick wall, his legs were taken from under him as his arms were pinned to his sides, just as a large hand was clamped over his mouth. He felt himself being dumped onto the ground as all of the air was driven from his chest. A piece of cloth was stuffed into his mouth as a gag. His eyes were covered with sticky black tape and his hands and feet were expertly bound. Then he felt himself being lifted up and carried to a nearby waiting vehicle where he was thrown in. All of this was done in a total and unnerving silence.

At about 2315hrs the major's land-rover arrived at the camp. On being told he wasn't needed, the driver returned to barracks, more than a little put out on a wasted trip.


At 0530hrs Dacre, Taylor and Corporal McBride had all the recruits awake and up. Fires were lit and water was put on for coffee and a shave. Recruit Ackland and his two oppos had discretely disappeared to check their snares. They now stood in front of Dacre and their squad instructor proudly holding two dead rabbits apiece. Even Dacre was surprised by their success.

"Well, young Ackland, what can I say but well done! You must have been a bloody good gamekeeper. Clearly the Duke of Devonshire's loss has been a gain for Her Majestys Royal Marines. I suggest that your Corporal arranges for you and your mates to present them to the major when we get back, he should be delighted with such initiative. For the next half hour there was battle PT for everyone. Just as they finished, a land-rover drove into the field. For one moment the corporal thought it was the major returning as promised.

"Is that the major?"

"I very much doubt it," said Dacre with a slight smile on his face.

At that moment a laughing Pincher Martin jumped out of the vehicle followed by the other pioneers.

"Gather around, boys and girls, Uncle James has brought you breakfast!" Unhooking the tailgate to the vehicle he revealed two urns of hot tea and coffee and dozens of brown paper bags, each one containing a 'packed breakfast'.

"Well done, Pincher," said Dacre, "Just what we needed." Then as an aside, "How did it go?"

"Safely delivered to the Officer's Mess at 0500hrs this morning and no one saw us!"


After a much needed breakfast, the squad cleared the field, so well in fact that it would have been difficult to tell that anyone had been there, let alone over sixty men camping rough. They lined up in three ranks and then doubled marched back to barracks, with the land-rover bringing up the rear. Just before they came into Walmer, Dacre suggested that they stop and get themselves squared away. Each man brushed down his neighbour, blue berets were straightened and fighting orders were adjusted. Corporal McBride spoke.

"Now then lads, let's have a bit of swank as we march in, shall we, heels down, arms in line with the shoulders, eyes to the front, nice and crisp like! Let's show them we are as good if not better than most!" As they approached the main entrance, the duty sentry had swung open the heavy main gates. He just stood and stared in utter amazement as the squad marched in, perfect in every detail and a fine example of what good Royal Marines should be.


Later that morning Dacre received a message that the RSM wanted to see him right away. He wasn't that perturbed since he had been half expecting the summons. Standing in front of the RSM's desk, Dacre could see from the grim expression on his face that the RSM was not a happy man.

"Right! I have just spent a very unpleasant half an hour with the CO and the second in command. Major Blair is absolutely livid and wants blood, yours mine or anyone's will do. He is demanding an investigation and court marshals left, right and centre. And to top it all a couple of recruits have brought him half a dozen dead rabbits. Luckily it was the Mess Sergeant who found him, trussed up like a bloody chicken, so at least he'll keep his mouth shut. I've already spoken to Corporal McBride and several of his section commanders who all assure me that you were with them last night. And surprise, surprise all of the remainder of the Pioneers seem to have watertight alibis. So, much against my better judgment I shall be advising the Brigadier that there appears to be insufficient evidence to take this matter any further. Just remember this, there are some things which aren't acceptable. So never again! Do you hear me? Never again! I hope I make myself absolutely clear!"

"Yes Sir! Absolutely clear!"

"That's all. Now get the hell out of here!" Dacre turned to open the door.

"AJ?"

"Sir?"

"Bloody well done!" A small smile had momentarily crossed the RSM's face.

"Sir!"

# 22

BRIGADIER Ellis listened carefully to the instructions he was being given by the Private Secretary from the Prime Minister's office, he made an occasional note on the pad in front of him.

"Right Sir, I understand. I'll see to it straight away." With that, he hung up the phone, then he pressed his intercom switch, "Petty Officer Kelly, will you get the RSM to come and see me straight away."

"Aye, aye Sir, straight away!"

The Brigadier sat staring at the fireplace, deep in thought. Only he and the RSM new that of the three Brunei sailors undergoing a crash course in marine training, the youngest was in fact the Sultan's only son, the crown prince. He and his two bodyguards actually were navy, but it had been thought by those in authority, that his real identity should be kept secret. Whilst waiting for the RSM to arrive, the Brigadier took the opportunity to refresh his memory about the links between Brunei and the Britain. The Foreign Office at the request of the MOD had thoughtfully produced a very useful summary. Opening the folder, he began to read:

+ *Britain has a long-standing political and economic relationship with the small Islamic Sultanate in the north-west corner of the island of Borneo.*

+ *Brunei is an absolute monarchy, where the Sultan rules by decree. He is the $28^{th}$ ruler in line going back over six hundred years. The Sultan is the richest man in the world.*

+ *Islam came to Brunei during the mid $15^{th}$ century after wealthy Muslim families fled Malacca following the arrival of the Portuguese.*

+ Brunei has an illustrious past and was at its height in the $16^{th}$ century. When the first Europeans arrived in 1521, they found a splendid and sophisticated royal court.

+ The country's wealth at that time was in the main due to its lucrative control over the merchant traffic in the South China Sea.

+ By the end of the $16^{th}$ century, Spain was exploring the region with a view to further colonisation. Following a sea battle which the Spanish won, they occupied Brunei's capital, only to leave it a couple of days later because of an outbreak of cholera.

+ By the end of the $19^{th}$ century, trade had declined and local piracy increased. This together with internal strife led the western entrepreneurs arriving to take advantage of the situation, most notably Britain.

+ In 1839, James Brooke helped the Sultan put down an uprising. In return, Brooke demanded and was given the governorship of Sarawak. He used the suppression of piracy as an excuse to siphon off more and more territory.

+ In 1846, another internal coup was quelled by British gunboats, in which Royal Marines played a key role. This led to a treaty forbidding the Sultanate from ceding any of its territories without British consent.

+ By 1888, Britain had declared Brunei a 'protected state', thus the responsibility for all of the country's foreign affairs lay with London.

+ At the beginning of the $20^{th}$ century oil was discovered. The British then set up a 'Residency'.

+ By 1931, oil was flowing freely and the profits allowed Brunei to pay off its many debts from the lean years of the 19th century. Britain of course also took a healthy slice of the profits.

+ In 1941, the Japanese invasion halted Brunei's recovery. The occupation lasted three and a half years.

+ In the post war years, other regions such as Sabah and Sarawak became Crown Colonies. Brunei, however, remained a British Protectorate with its British Resident.

+ In 1959, the Residency was withdrawn and a new constitution established. The Sultan was very careful to retain British involvement in matters of defence and foreign affairs.

+ Both the Sultan and his son the crown prince had been educated in Britain and Malaya. The Sultan is particularly keen *on his son receiving a military training that can then be replicated in Brunei.*

*NOTE: the current geopolitical situation with regard to President Sukarno of Indonesia and his policy on expansionism in the Far East (he has publically declared his intention to take over the rest of Borneo, then Malaya and Singapore) means that a Federation of Malaysia (Malaya, Sabah, Sarawak and Singapore) is now more likely. Whether or not Brunei will join this Federation is as yet undecided.*

The Brigadier frowned. It was he thought a wonder that a country like Brunei that had been so exploited over the years by the British still looked to Britain for help.

The RSM knocked and entered the CO's office.

"Ah, Mr McFee. Our young prince is to meet with his father on the 23$^{rd}$ April in the morning. It appears that the Sultan is making an unofficial visit to this country and would like to see his one and only. The Prime Minister's Office has arranged for them to use Allington Castle, which I understand is located just outside Maidstone; it's discreet and out of the way. The prince and his two bodyguards are to travel up the night before in civvies and are to stay over. They can use my staff car, perhaps you will ask my driver if he will do the trip."

"Right Sir, I'll see to that!"

"I assume Mr McFee that the Prince's two men are armed?"

"I believe so Sir, side arms, although I have never actually asked." The CO nodded.

"How are the Pioneers getting on with their training? Is the Badge pushing them too hard or not hard enough?"

"Oh, they are making good progress, Sir, toughening up nicely. I had thought he might be too severe for them, but they all seem to have responded well, they really are working like a team, if you know what I mean, notwithstanding our recent upset with the major"

"Well, let's not go into that business, shall we. The sooner that's forgotten the better."

"Yes, Sir, I quite agree. Anyway they are out and about today brushing up on their radio procedures."

"Good, I'm glad things are going well, clearly Dacre was the right man for the job." The RSM simply nodded.

"Okay, Mr McFee, that will be all."

"Sir!"

The following morning Dacre AJ was making his weekly report to the RSM.

"Morning AJ."

"Morning Sir!"

"All going well?" Dacre confirmed that it was and gave a brief but detailed sitrep on the progress the Pioneers were making.

"That sounds good to me. I was only telling the CO what good progress the lads were making. Out and about yesterday?"

"Yes Sir. Just brushing up on our radio procedures. I thought the Section deserved something less demanding, I've been pushing them pretty hard lately."

"Around locally, were you?" asked the RSM. Dacre wondered where this conversation was going.

"Yes Sir, down on the beach and around the roads nearby."

"Ever Heard of '*Watch with Mother*'?"

"Sir?"

"It's a television programme for little children. It's usually broadcast about 2.00 o'clock in the afternoon. The usual characters are *Andy Pandy and his friends Teddy and Looby Lu.*"

"Sir?"

"Apparently part way through yesterday's programme, Teddy told his friend Andy Pandy that he was fed up with playing these games and he was going for a cup of fucking tea!" Here the RSM paused. Dacre was stunned into silence. Never in his wildest moments could he ever have thought of something like this happening, he was horrified. The RSM continued.

"I have received numerous complaints from local mothers who have asked if we are responsible. According to the Signals Officer, the frequency that the BBC uses to transmit their programmes on is very similar to that being used by the military, that is us. So much so that it is quite possible to interrupt a television programme if we are transmitting close by at the same time."

"Yes Sir, I understand completely," said Dacre quietly.

"So AJ, I would appreciate it that in future your lads kept to the correct radio procedure."

"Yes Sir! Thank you Sir! I'm sure the lads will be terribly upset when I tell them. I'll make sure it never happens again."

"Yes, well, I'm sure they will be upset. Just remind them we have only just got over the swearing business. Okay, that's all for now AJ. Remember what I said, we don't want any more interruptions to children's television, do we?"

"No sir!"

# 23

ALLINGTON Castle lies two miles to the north-west of Maidstone, the county town of Kent. The castle was originally built in 1281; it was later converted to a fortified house in the 15$^{th}$ century. About 1600, a fire reduced the castle to a shell until about 1905 when it was bought and restored by the explorer Sir Martin Conway. In 1951, the castle was taken over by the Carmelite Order based at nearby Aylesford.

The military police land-rover turned off the main London Road into a narrow lane that meandered through typical Kentish orchards, down towards the River Medway. Arriving at the castle's gates, the vehicle stopped in front of the old barbican drawbridge. A sergeant got out and walked up to the heavy wooden gates and pulled a bell rope. Somewhere inside, a mournful toll could be heard. After a few minutes, a small grill opened in a side door and an elderly but kindly be-whiskered face appeared. The sergeant held up his warrant card.

"Afternoon brother. We're the extra security for your special visitor!" The monk looked past the sergeant to the waiting land-rover.

"The prince isn't due until 7.00 o'clock this evening, but never mind, you had better come in." He began undoing the large iron bolts that held the heavy gates in place.

"Let me give you a hand," said the sergeant, waving the vehicle forward. Once everyone was inside and the gates were closed, the sergeant detailed four of his men to various strategic points around the castle. The brother watched this deployment with a mixture of admiration and apprehension. As a Carmelite from the nearby priory, his forty years had taught him, amongst many other things, the need for efficiency. He was, however, less happy with all the weapons that these soldiers were carrying. But, always a practical man, he reasoned needs must.

"Now then, brother, perhaps you could gather the castle staff for me in the kitchen."

"Yes, of course. There is only the housekeeper and her husband, both are elderly. They live in and have rooms over the old pantry." The brother led the way across the gravelled courtyard, his long brown robes flapping in the wind. The sergeant turned to the remaining soldier.

"Right Seamus, you know what to do. Put all three of them in the buttery and make sure they have food and water and they are nice and secure. Then come across and join me in the Penchester Room."

"Okay, Padraig, I'll see they give us no trouble."

"In the meantime, I'm going to check out that the lads are all in position."


At precisely 7.00 p.m., a dark green staff car drew up at the castle gates. The driver flashed his headlights and, as the gates opened, he drove into the courtyard. Seeing the military police vehicle, the driver half turned his head towards those in the back seat.

"Looks like some extra security for you, Sir." Having parked the car, Marine West got out. He went to open the rear door. As he did so, he was vaguely aware of some movement behind him, when there was for a split second a blinding flash of light and a most horrendous pain to the left side of his head. He sank slowly to his knees and then toppled forward onto the gravel, unconscious and totally oblivious to the small stones and pebbles that gouged and tore into his face. In the rear seat, the two bodyguards seeing what had happened to their driver tried to draw their weapons; they were too late. On each side of the car, a military policeman with a silenced pistol, expertly and effectively fired three shots into each guard, two to the chest and one to the head.

"Get the prince into the building," growled Padraig. "Leave the bodies in the car. If the driver is still alive, put him in the buttery with the others and check he is not armed."

"I'll need some help. He's a big bastard and no mistake!"

In any other circumstances, the Penchester Room would have been very comfortable. It had a high ceiling and panelled walls, which were ornamented by numerous paintings and coats of arms. The floor was covered in rush matting and a log fire was ablaze in a large inglenook fireplace. The prince was seated in an upright wooden armchair, his arms and wrists securely tied to the arm rests. Despite looking pale and shocked, he stared defiantly at his two captors.

"Alright, Seamus, a little finger will do!" The prince could not see the wire cutters. His left hand was held in a vice-like grip. Suddenly, there was a most terrible pain in his left hand, a pain that shot up his arm to his shoulder that made him scream out loud. The soldier held up the bleeding hand and clumsily wrapped a bandage around the severed stump of the little finger. The pain was unbelievable, he felt faint and wanted to be sick; he gritted his teeth together in an effort to remain conscious. Seamus picked up the amputated finger and put it into a match box.

"I'll take this down to the main gate then. They should be here soon enough."

"Alright, then on the way back check on the boys up top, will you, and remind them to keep a sharp lookout, we're in for a long wait! Tell them we'll sort out some food and hot drinks later."

# 24

THE highly polished black limousine drove into the secluded forecourt of a Ministry of Defence building just off Whitehall in London. Other than the letters RN on the number plate, there was no indication that this was a military vehicle. The Royal Marine driver and his two passengers were dressed in civilian clothes. A presentation to the Minister of Defence, Harold Watkinson at his suggestion and the Joint Chiefs of Staff was scheduled for precisely 20.00hrs.

Major General James L Moulton RM, Chief of Amphibious Warfare, and his colleague and long-standing friend, Brigadier General Eugene Fornadley USMC, had a difficult task ahead of them. After several years of hard work, they had yet to convince the Chiefs of Staff that the future of amphibious forces lay in the need for two LPDs. The recent success of the conversation of the two light fleet carriers HMS Albion and HMS Bulwark into commando carriers or LPHs gave them some hope of a successful outcome, but nothing was certain.

At about 21.15 hrs, the highly charged meeting had taken a short break for coffee. The three single service chiefs were proving to be quite stubborn. The Army continued to focus all of their energies on the British Army on the Rhine, whilst the Royal Navy saw anti-submarine warfare in the North Atlantic as their main priority. The Royal Air Force were totally absorbed with their 'V' Bombers. Consequently, there was little or no interest in the idea of Amphibious Warfare, with the possible exception of the Fleet Air Arm who saw the deployment of helicopters to their advantage. General Fornadley's thirty minute presentation on how the USMC was actually developing amphibious warfare had clearly impressed and even shocked the Joint Chiefs; they were completely unaware of the modern technology being used. Even Lord Louis Mountbatten, who had been one of the most difficult to convince, seemed to be more than just interested. Just as the meeting reassembled with the Minister calling them to order, a red phone in the corner of the room gave a sharp ring. One of the aides walked across the room to answer it. As he listened, he looked towards the Minister.

"It's for you Sir! It's the Home Secretary, there has been an incident!" The Minister took the phone, he noticed that his hand was sweating slightly.

"Harold here, Charles." He listened carefully for several minutes, nodding his head in agreement.

"Right Charles, I have the picture, leave this with me. I will come back to you as soon as possible, certainly within the next half-hour." Putting the phone down he turned towards the assembled group of officers. The room was silent; there was an air of expectation.

"Gentlemen, I have to inform you that the Crown Prince of Brunei has been kidnapped and at this very moment is being held captive just outside Maidstone. A ransom of £100,000 has been demanded and must be delivered by the Sultan himself by 2.00 a.m. tomorrow morning. The caller was Irish and gave the appropriate code to show that this is a legitimate IRA operation. As a sign of the kidnapper's intent, the local police have received a severed finger believed to belong to the prince." The room was immediately full of the buzz of animated and angry voices. The Minister had to raise his voice to be heard.

"Gentlemen! You also need to know that the Sultan is due to arrive in the UK at 11.30 p.m. tonight. He is on an unofficial visit to request military help against the continuing unrest and communist-inspired activity in his country; particularly since President Surkarno of Indonesia is backing the local guerrillas as part of his plans for taking over the rest of Borneo. The Sultan was going to meet up with his son, who is currently undergoing some training with the Royal Marines at Deal. The government has agreed to this meeting and has made Allington Castle available to them, which is where the prince is now being held."

The Minister paused and looked around the table at the faces of the most senior military officers in the country. Not one showed any emotion. He continued.

"Resolving the situation is beyond the local constabulary, good as they are. So the Home Secretary has asked for military help. Reluctantly, the Prime Minister has agreed. So I propose we suspend the original purpose of our meeting and consider what options we have available, especially as time is of the essence."

Almost immediately, Lord Mountbatten, a long-time supporter of the Royal Marines, cleared his throat in order to attract attention.

"Sir, with all due respect to my colleagues may I suggest that we keep this a navy matter, or to be more precise a Royal Marines matter." The Minister looked around the table. Charles Lamb, the First Sea Lord nodded his head in agreement. The Minister looked at the Chief of the Imperial Staff, Frank Festing. He agreed as did the Vice Chief of the Air Staff. Mountbatten continued.

"Thank you, Sir. Perhaps we could begin by asking General Moulton to share with us his current knowledge regarding Royal Marines Commando forces in the UK at this moment in time. General?" Moulton leant forward to take a sip of his now cold coffee, anything to buy himself a few precious seconds of thinking time. As CAW he had no direct responsibility for the deployment of troops either in the UK or abroad. However, having recently been MGRM Portsmouth and with an eye on amphibious developments, he still made it his business to have a working knowledge of what was going on in the Corps. Looking around at the assembled faces, he took a slow deep breath to help him relax.

"Sir. To the best of my knowledge the situation here in the UK is as follows: 43 Commando RM from Plymouth are on their way to Aden embarked on HMS Albion, there to join up with 40 and 42 Commando. 41 Commando RM from Bickleigh have several companies training in Scotland. Our SBS unit from JSWAC Poole are in Malta along with several troops of the SAS. At RM Barracks Eastney we have several ships' companies undergoing pre-embarkation training. In addition, others are being trained as signallers and cooks. At Fort Cumberland driver training continues as usual. There is also a new Royal Marines Provost course underway, partly delivered by ourselves and by the Royal Military Police at their barracks in Chichester. In reality, that leaves just the two training establishments: ITCRM at Lympstone and The Depot at Deal. Whilst both of these are concerned with the training of recruits, they will have a number of highly qualified instructors. However, it seems to me that they would not be able to provide the sort of small specialist team that we are looking for to carry out this rescue. Lympstone would be the best place to look since they are responsible for commando training. But they are too far away and it would take too long to assemble a team. In short, although The Depot is the nearest, it is also the least likely to be able to help. So as much as I regret this, we may have to ask the army for some help." He paused to let his words sink in. He continued.

"There are garrisons at Dover and Canterbury and there are troops at Maidstone and Chatham." Mountbatten got to his feet.

"Thank you General for your appraisal, that was most illuminating!" Then looking at the First Sea Lord he said,

"I'm damned if we are going to the army yet!"

Turning to the Minister,

"With your permission, Sir?" Harold Watkinson waved carry on.

"General, who is the commanding officer at Deal?"

"Brigadier Graham Ellis, Sir."

"Right, phone him now, explain the situation briefly and let's see what he can do."

General Moulton looked to the Minister for confirmation, who nodded an agreement. The General went across to the phone, picked up the receiver and asked for a line. He was connected immediately.

"Good evening, Graham, James Moulton here. Listen carefully. We have a situation and need some help." After five minutes, he put the phone back down. He turned to the assembled company.

"As I half expected. He has plenty of instructors, but nothing that we could use." Mountbatten let out an exasperated expletive. Silence descended on the group, each person in the room coming to terms with the news. Suddenly, the phone rang again. An Aide answered it.

"It's Brigadier Ellis, he wants to speak to the General." He took the phone and listened intently for several minutes.

"Right! Good! Thank you, Graham. Have someone stay by the telephone, I will come back to as quickly as I can." He replaced the phone, a smile spreading across his face as he turned to the others. Well, gentlemen, someone up there would seem to love us! It appears that a small group of marines at The Depot have been training for the past six weeks for a competition. They are supremely fit and are weapon and canoe trained. The RSM rates them as some of the toughest men in the Corps and they are led by one, Marine Dacre AJ."

The Minister looked aghast.

"You are surely not suggesting that we entrust this mission to a mere marine, surely?" Mountbatten and the First Sea Lord looked quizzically at Moulton. The general looked directly at Harold Watkinson. He felt himself begin to flush with a rising sense of anger, he struggled to keep his voice calm.

"Sir! With all due respect, this marine served with me in 48 Commando RM for two years, including D-Day and Normandy. He was promoted to Acting Sergeant in the field and later commissioned to Captain as a Troop Commander, when all of his officers were either killed or wounded. He is also SBS-trained and has seen service all over the world. He is the most highly decorated marine in the Corps, in short he is a marine's marine. His small team consists of experts in small arms, explosives, canoe work and unarmed combat. If anyone can rescue the prince, he and his team can!" The Minister sat still for a moment or two taking in all of this information. Why he wondered was this man still only in the ranks. Surely if he was that good he should have been a senior officer by now. He decided not to ask the question, besides what other choice did he have? The First Sea Lord was smiling.

"Well, General, how soon can this team be operational and how do we get them there?"

"They can be ready to go within an hour or so, how we get them there is another matter. It would be two hours or more by road and then they would have to deploy." One of the aides spoke up.

"There is Manston Airport, Sir."

"What do you mean?" asked Lord Mountbatten.

"Well, Sir, although the Americans are no longer based there, I believe the RAF does have an air-sea rescue unit there and they will have helicopters." Moulton thought about this piece of information, his experience as a pilot coming to the fore.

"That's it! Flying time from Manston to Deal, say ten minutes. They can land on the cricket pitch in front of the officer's mess. Then pick up our team and fly them up to Maidstone, maybe another thirty minutes or so. That means they could be deployed within an hour, all being well." For the first time the Minister looked happy.

"What about getting them out, General?"

"I think, Sir, we had better leave that to Dacre and his team, don't you?"

"Yes! Yes, of course, you are quite right."

"There is one thing, Sir, that we need to get clear though, rules of engagement!"

"What? Oh yes, of course, well …" Mountbatten interrupted.

"If I may suggest, Sir? We are dealing with an armed group who has kidnapped a visiting person of royalty, who is or rather was under our protection. I suggest we treat this as an act of war and act accordingly." The Minister thought about this.

"My instinct is to do as you suggest, but I need to clear this with the Prime Minister." Three minutes later, Harold Watkinson was back at the table.

"The PM agrees with us, but stipulates the minimum amount of force necessary to secure the release of the Crown Prince. General, will you liaise with the CO at The Depot, I will personally see to the helicopters. What time do we want them to arrive?" Everyone in the conference room looked at their watches.

"I have 21.45 hours," said the First Sea Lord.

"Let's say 23.30 is the start time," replied Moulton.

"Agreed!" said the Minister. "Is that all?" One of the Naval aides spoke up.

"Sir. We do need a code word for this operation. May I suggest that since tomorrow is the 23rd of April, perhaps we might use Saint George?" The Minister looked puzzled. Lord Mountbatten and the First Sea Lord both looked at General Moulton, they were smiling broadly.

"Of course St George's Day and the Battle of Zeebrugge 1918. Thank you, what an excellent idea. If no one objects, then *Operation Saint George* it is."


Later as they were being driven away, Major General Moulton broke into a deep chuckle. His friend looked at him sideways.

"I didn't have the heart to tell their lordships that this specialist team we are about to deploy is in fact The Depot's very own Pioneer Section." There was a sharp intake of breath from his companion as the significance of what he had just said sank in.

"I hope to goodness your marine can deliver then!"

"So do I, Gene, so do I!"

# 25

BRIGADIER Graham Ellis MC RM, as the Commanding Officer and guest of honour, sat at the head of the dining table in the officer's mess. The table had been meticulously laid for thirty officers, all of whom were in formal mess dress. The silverware and table centres sparkled under the lights of the chandeliers; it was as it should be on this very grand and special occasion. In the Corps, Zeebrugge Day, which commemorates the raid by marines and sailors on the heavily defended German-held harbour in 1918, is celebrated on St George's Day. However, at The Depot this commemoration actually takes place on the evening of the 22$^{nd}$ April, the night before the raid, since that was the last meal served to the 4$^{th}$ Battalion RM. A similar formal dinner was also taking place in the Sergeant's Mess and to a lesser extent in the main dining hall.

A MOA appeared discretely at the Brigadier's elbow.

"Sir, there is a phone call for you from Whitehall. Major General Moulton needs to speak to you most urgently." The Brigadier got up from his chair quickly and made his way to the nearby anti-room, he picked up the receiver and listened intently.

"I understand what you are asking for, James, and even though the prince is temporarily one of mine, I'm afraid we have nothing here that would suit your needs. I'm terribly sorry, I wish you luck elsewhere." Putting the phone down he made his way slowly back to the dining room deep in thought. He was shocked to hear what had happened to his young prince, now in the hands of the IRA. Stopping in mid stride, he spun around, his face lighting up, quickly he retrieved the phone.

"Put me through to the RSM immediately!" A hasty conversation followed.

"Thank you, Mr McFee. I'll get back to the General at once, oh and you had better round everybody up. Let's say 'O' group in my office in fifteen minutes." The switchboard reconnected the Brigadier with General Moulton straight away.

The CO's office was extremely crowded. All of the pioneers and the RSM were trying to look at an OS map spread out on the desk. Formalities and rank had for the moment been put to one side. The Brigadier finished his appraisal of the situation.

"The Chief Constable will be sending further details and maps of Allington Castle by a police motor cyclist, he should be here by 2245hrs." At that precise moment, the door to the office was thrown open as the second in command came storming in, everyone looked up.

"Sir! I have just heard the news and what is being proposed. I really must protest!" Brigadier Ellis raised his hand to stop the major's outburst, but Major Blair wasn't in the mood to be stopped, he continued.

"You can't possibly allow this important mission to be entrusted to a mere marine and this bunch of inadequates!" Here he paused and looked around the room as if to emphasise the point.

"There needs to be a senior officer in command, someone who can fully appreciate the international sensitivity of the situation." The room had gone very quiet, all eyes were on the major. It was obvious to everyone that he had been drinking and perhaps more to the point how did he find out what was happening?

"Are you volunteering, Major Blair?" The Brigadier's tone was icy.

"Well, not exactly, I wasn't thinking of myself, perhaps someone else."

"Thank you, Major!" The CO paused for effect. "However, General Moulton has specifically asked for Marine Dacre and his team to undertake this operation, so there is nothing more to be discussed, is there?" The major shuffled uneasily from foot to foot. He went red in the face from embarrassment and from the fact that both he and everyone else in the room knew that he had been outflanked as well as outranked.

Ignoring the major, who had now retreated to a corner, the Brigadier turned to Dacre AJ.

"You and your team have about an hour or so to get ready. Two helicopters from Manston will arrive at 2330hrs to airlift you to Maidstone." The marine nodded.

"I know this area quite well. We can be dropped off here at Allington Lock, we can then paddle upstream to the castle and be in position ready to assault by 0100hrs. What we really need is some sort of a diversion, something that will bring the guards to the front of the castle and away from the river, something biggish but not too obvious." The Brigadier looked at the marine.

"What do you have in mind, Badge?"

Dacre looked carefully at the map.

"Maybe a fire up by the tarmacadum works, a shed or old garage would do, something that will make a good blaze." The Brigadier smiled, all the others with the exception of the major nodded in approval.

"I'll speak to the Chief Constable. He's offered what help he can."

"If I may, Sir, I would like to study the map some more. I'll leave Marine Martin to sort out the Section and get them ready. Perhaps the RSM would look after the ammunition and grenades. Apart from our personal weapons we had better have a Bren gun and a two-inch mortar with both HE and smoke bombs. I would like everyone back here at 2300hrs, fully booted and spurred for a final briefing and hopefully going over the plans of the castle."

After everyone had left the office, Brigadier Ellis decided to raise the question that so far, no one had wanted to ask.

"Assuming that you can get to the Sultan's son, how are you going to get him away?" Dacre AJ paused before answering.

"I'm not really sure, Sir. Since these are IRA 'soldiers', their planning will be good. They are bound to have at least one, maybe even two back-up teams nearby. So simply driving out will not be an option. Since we are going in by river, that would seem to be our obvious way out, at least back to the lock. I had thought we could simply radio for the helicopters and they could airlift us out. But, to be honest, it will be impossible to arrange a safe rendezvous since the two helicopters circling overhead would not only give our position away, but would make for easy targets for the IRA. So I think we will have to rely on our own initiative to get us away safely. Perhaps the police could be asked to leave us a car at the lock, that would give us an option." The Brigadier looked at the marine with a real sense of respect.

"Do you think you can pull this off, Badge?" He asked quietly.

"Well, the physical and mental state of the Section is good, in fact far superior to most. If you remember the old maxim about a well-planned and well led attack, then I believe these marines will not only go the distance but will keep on going, because that is what they have been trained to do. So, we will do our utmost to get the prince back." With that, he went back to studying the map; several ideas were already beginning to form in his mind. Later, when the Brigadier left the office, Dacre AJ made a phone call to his old sailing friend Dick Browning in Whitstable.

"Dick, AJ here. I need some information from you and a favour…"


Back in his office, Major Blair was beside himself with anger and the humiliation he had suffered at the hands of that so-called marine's marine. There was nothing he could do to alter the situation, but he would have his revenge, somehow, somewhere. He needed a distraction urgently, something that would take his mind off the last hour. He reached for the phone.

"Put me through to the WRNS quarters, will you!" he snapped. The exchange connected him almost immediately.

"Petty Officer Kelly please? Ah, PO can you bring file 69 to my office now! Yes, I know it's late, but I need that file right now!" There was long pause on the other end of the line.

"I'm sorry, Sir, that particular file is no longer available."

"What?"

"Yes, Sir! It's been withdrawn permanently!" With that the phone went dead. The major sat very still, the anger welling up inside him like a volcano. Then, with one swift movement he swept everything off his desk onto the floor with an almighty crash. He looked at the pile of debris on the floor rather like a petulant child who has had his sweets taken away from him. You couldn't rely on anyone these days, he thought. In her small bedroom, PO Sue Kelly sat on the edge of her bed, tears rolling down her cheeks. As soon as she had heard his voice on the phone, she experienced the old weakening sensation that overcame her when in his presence. It had not been an easy decision to make, but she felt sure it was the right one.

At precisely 2300hrs, the marines reassembled in the CO's office. Dacre AJ spread out the plans of the castle, which, although were old, circa 1905, he hoped would serve their purpose. Quickly he ran through the key features and outlined his proposed plan of action. The marines listened intently to the instructions and studied the map carefully, each of them knowing that their lives might depend on this knowledge. The Brigadier and the RSM watched with admiration. Finally, the CO said,

"Badge, one last thing. The Sultan is due to deliver the ransom at 0300hrs. How will you let us know the situation?"

"Well, Sir, I am assuming that the telephones won't be working, so we are taking an R42 radio. We'll use the operational code word 'George' as our call sign, you'll be 'sunray', I assume?" The Brigadier nodded in agreement. Dacre continued.

"We will radio in a SITREP as soon as we can. If for any reason the radios don't work, then we will use a verey pistol as back-up; green will mean that we have the prince and are away. If it is red, that will mean we have failed and the ransom must be delivered."

# PART TWO

*Per Mare Per Terram*

(By Sea by Land)

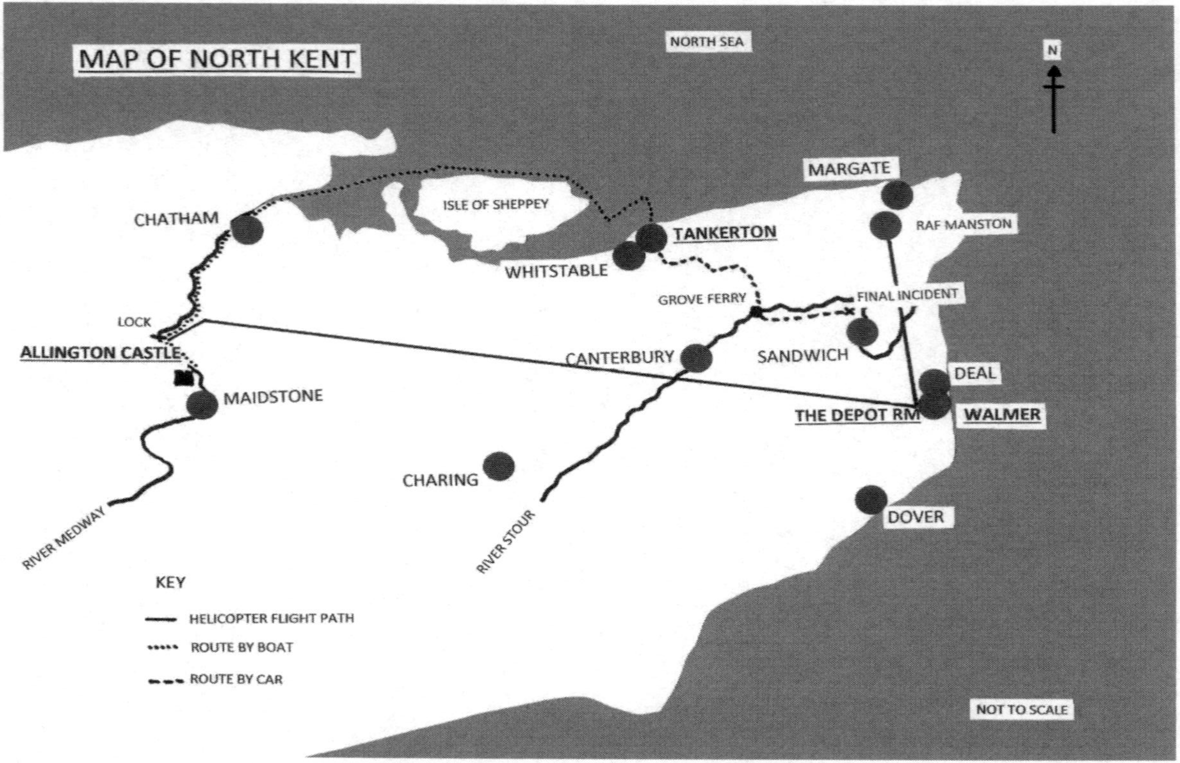
MAP OF NORTH KENT
NORTH SEA
N
MARGATE
RAF MANSTON
ISLE OF SHEPPEY
CHATHAM
TANKERTON
WHITSTABLE
GROVE FERRY
FINAL INCIDENT
LOCK
ALLINGTON CASTLE
CANTERBURY
SANDWICH
DEAL
THE DEPOT RM
WALMER
MAIDSTONE
CHARING
DOVER
RIVER MEDWAY
RIVER STOUR
KEY
HELICOPTER FLIGHT PATH
ROUTE BY BOAT
ROUTE BY CAR
NOT TO SCALE

# 26

AT precisely 2330hrs, the two Air-Sea Rescue helicopters from RAF Manston touched down, side by side on the cricket pitch in front of the officer's mess. The noise was deafening and many lights in the nearby homes of the residents of Walmer were switched on, with just as many curses, 'what the hell is going on?' Dacre AJ and his marines were waiting, kneeling in two sticks, fully armed, faces blackened, with all of their equipment, ready to go. They embarked swiftly and the two helicopters lifted off together, their navigation lights flashing in the darkness; they had not been on the ground for more than a minute. The Brigadier and the RSM stood watching until the helicopter's lights had disappeared from sight.

"There is nothing more we can do tonight, Mr McFee, we might as well turn in and get what sleep we can, goodness knows what tomorrow will bring."

"Yes, Sir. I'll make sure that the Duty NCO and the Guard Commander are on the alert. I presume the Signal's Officer and his team will be on watch throughout the night?"

"Yes, I have personally made sure of that. They are to report to me immediately if and when any signal comes through."

"That other business tonight with the second-in-command. He simply asked the switchboard what was going on. They in all innocence told him." The CO just grunted.

"I'll wish you good night then, Sir." The Brigadier nodded, but remained silently looking into the night sky. The RSM took the hint and left quietly, walking across the grass to the SNCO's mess.

Aboard the lead helicopter Dacre took the headset offered to him by the crewman. He spoke clearly and slowly into the mouthpiece.

"Follow the North Downs to a point where the River Medway cuts through the chalk hills. Make a ninety degree turn at the new bridge, out navigation lights, then follow the river inland until you reach the lock. There should be a small car park on your port side, grid reference 749582. Roger that?"

"Roger that, wilco, out!" came the reply. The pilot turned to his co-pilot.

"I suppose it's better we don't know what is going on. But these commando chaps give me the willies, talk about a mean looking bunch. I wouldn't want to tangle with them."

Twenty minutes later, the two helicopters touched down in turn, unloaded the men and their equipment and were off back to their base, the sound of the rota blades disappearing into the night. The small group of marines sprang into action, assembling the three canoes in less than five minutes. Weapons and bergans were loaded on board and the canoes were in the water ready to go. Dacre called Tubby Taylor over to confirm his earlier briefing.

"You know what to do. Liberate a nice fast launch and make sure there is plenty of fuel. Collect the canoes from where we leave them and have the Bren gun ready in case we need covering fire on leaving."

"You can rely on me, AJ, good luck!" Dacre climbed into his canoe. It was too dark for Taylor to wave them off, but he could just make out their white teeth, set in their blackened faces grinning at him as they paddled away.

It took just fifteen minutes paddling at an easy rate to arrive at the castle. Although the night was dark, the silhouette of the $12^{th}$ century fortress was even darker. Securing the canoes to the river bank, the marines disembarked, put on their bergans and put a round up the spout in their weapons. At Dacre's whispered command, they spread out into an extended line and began to move slowly and carefully forward through the waist-high grass towards the castle, until they reached the edge of the moat.

Wrapping their waterproof capes around their packs, each marine made a watertight float. Silently, they slipped into the cold water and, taking care not to disturb any sleeping waterfowl, they swam across. Dacre was the first to land on the narrow ledge of grass at the foot of a garden wall. Several minutes later, they were all over and across the gardens hugging the foot of the high castle wall. Dacre had already attached a climbing rope to his waist, ready to free climb to the top. Taking care not to be seen from above, he checked the luminous dial of his watch. Beside him the other marines were huddled together, the water had been bitterly cold and with the cool wind several sets of teeth were beginning to chatter. Dacre checked his watch again, 'come on come on', he thought, 'we haven't got all night.' Suddenly from high above them, the marines distinctly heard an Irish voice call out.

"Hey, Liam! Will you come and look at this. Some sort of a fire, jeez that's big."

"Alright, alright, I'm coming." Footsteps could be clearly heard moving along the battlements to the far side of the castle.

"Liam, you had better use the walkie-talkie to tell the boss. You know what the instructions are."

"Okay, okay!" Switching on the handset he spoke quickly into the mouthpiece.

"Padraig, it's me Liam. Look, there's a big fire, maybe half a mile away. You can hear the fire engines coming already, enough fucking bells to wake the dead!" He listened carefully to the reply, then switched off.

"The boss says keep a sharp lookout. It could be some sort of a diversion."

"Some fucking diversion! Give us a fag, will you, I'm freezing my bollocks off standing up here in the cold."

As soon as Dacre heard the distant sound of the fire engines, he began to climb the castle wall. By the time he had reached the battlements, the sweat was pouring off him and his heart was pounding. The knuckles of his hands, although well calloused with years of use, were raw and bleeding; the hand holds had been few and far between. He had needed all of his mountaineering skills to make the climb. He cautiously peered over the top, the fire could be seen in the distance. The silhouettes of the two guards on the far side of the castle clearly stood out. Dacre secured the rope and gave it two definite tugs. Within seconds, Geordie and Brum were alongside him, both were breathing heavily, the adrenalin coursing through their veins. Dacre simply pointed to the two guards. The two marines moved off silently along the battlements, keeping close to the cold damp walls. Below them, the courtyard was sporadically lit by the wall lights, creating pools of light inter-spaced by areas of pitch-black shadow. Gradually, the two marines edged their way forward step by step, their hearts beating so loudly surely someone must hear them. They stopped suddenly in mid-step, almost like in some grotesque dance. The guards had half turned towards them and were lighting cigarettes out of the wind. They straightened up and turned back to watch the fire. Geordie drew his commando knife silently from its leather sheath and signalled Brum to do the same. He shook his head and reached down to his waist belt, from where he pulled out a seven pound lump hammer. Keeping as close to the wall as possible, he moved towards the unsuspecting guards. Counting out the distance in his mind, Geordie took a deep breath and stood up. Using a not very convincing Irish accent, he called out,

"Have either of you'se two lads got a light?" The two guards spun around, startled, distracted, fumbling for their weapons, which were carelessly slung over their shoulders. At that moment, Brum stood up, all six foot four of him and fourteen stone, rising like a spectre of the night as if from nowhere. The guard nearest never knew what hit him as the marine brought the lump hammer down with all his might onto his head. There was a dull thud, the guard collapsed like a sack of potatoes, dead before he hit the ground. The second guard uttered a brief 'what the hell!' as Brum, turning lightly for such a big man, back swung the hammer up and under catching the Irishman directly on the chin, shattering the bone, driving shards up into the brain; death was instant. Geordie sprinted the last couple of steps just in time to catch the body as it slumped against the battlements. Both marines stood still looking at the corpses. Brum found he was shaking slightly, adrenalin or what? He had killed before, but always with a rifle and from a distance, never close up. He leant over the wall and was sick.

"You okay?" Geordie asked his friend.

"Yeh! Forget it!"

"Just look at these two, dressed like military police, cross belts the lot! What the fuck is going on here?"

"Dunno! Look I'll stay. You go and tell AJ that we are all clear here."

"Okay."

"Oh and Geordie, keep your head down." As the marine disappeared down into the darkness of the courtyard Brum pulled the two bodies to one side. From one he took a white cross belt and slipped it on, it might convince someone from a distance. From the other he took out some cigarettes and carefully lit one, he hadn't had a fag for years, but suddenly found he needed one. He noticed that his hands had stopped shaking.

# 27

Once Brum and Geordie had moved off, the other three marines joined Dacre on the ramparts. Placing his hand on Art Fagin's shoulder, he pointed towards the third guard whose silhouette was just visible far away in the south-west corner of the castle. Fagin moved off, crossing over the roof of the buttery and the kitchen. Using a short length of rope, which he secured, he eased himself down into the courtyard garden below where the foundations of the old castle could still be seen. Keeping close to the outer wall, he moved quickly and quietly to the tower with the spiral stairs that would take him up to the battlements. Cautiously, he made his way up to the top of the staircase. A military policeman, his back to the marine, was watching the fire in the distance. Fagin slipped out his commando knife, he paused then resheathed it. He realised here was a chance to really test himself. Over the years, he had trained hundreds of recruits in the necessary skills of fighting and killing with bare hands. Although he was a black belt in judo, he had never actually faced the ultimate challenge himself. This was his chance to prove to himself that he could actually deliver the goods. He would use his bare hands and his unarmed combat skills to do what needed to be done. Fagin stepped out onto the roof of the tower, cool and calm. He began to move, taking measured steps, almost in slow motion, silent and deadly, five or six paces to go. Something, maybe a sixth sense alerted the sentry. He turned quickly and brought his submachine gun up into the fire position. The marine reacted instinctively, he threw himself forward into a tight commando roll just as the silenced weapon was fired. Temporarily and partially blinded Fain automatically assumed the attack position. With his left hand he swept the gun aside, whilst he drove his right hand, fingers rigid, knife like, into the man's solar plexus. The guard was surprised by the ferocity of the attack, he was badly winded and hurt. Mustering all of his strength, he swung his weapon in an arc, up and then down on Fagin's left shoulder. The marine heard his collar bone break, the pain was unbelievable! Realising that he may have miscalculated, Fagin jammed two fingers of his right hand into his opponents eyes with all his might. The Irishman dropped his weapon and brought both hands up to his damaged eyes. The marine seized his opportunity; he brought his knee up into the man's groin, smashing his testicles in the process. With a high pitched squeal the Irishman doubled over. Using his good arm, the marine applied a headlock and then with one knee on the man's spine, threw all of his weight backward until he heard the spine snap. The encounter had been brief and brutal. Both men fell to the ground, the Irishman dead, the marine exhausted and hurting. Fagin lay still for a second or two, gathering what strength he had left. He pushed the body off himself and then fumbled around for his field dressing in order to make a temporary sling for his injured arm. Rolling onto his knees he searched around for his beret, he eventually found it, only to find a neat bullet hole just above his cap badge. What did they say about the commando green beret being bulletproof? So much for that myth! That had been close, too bloody close, he thought.

Almost immediately after Fagin had left, Dacre and Martin set off, also across the buttery and kitchen roof, leaving Timber Woods to safeguard their escape route. Martin continued along over the Long Gallery to a position above the steps that led up to the Penchester Room. Meanwhile, Dacre had climbed down into the courtyard by using a convenient drainpipe. Keeping close to the buildings and the darkness of the shadows, he made his way towards the parked vehicles, which he used as cover. Glancing in the staff car as he passed he saw the bodies of the two bodyguards, their dead eyes staring up blankly. He stiffened his shoulders; these Irishmen really were playing for keeps, so be it! Several things then happened in the space of the next few seconds. Dacre stepped out of the shadows in order to attract the attention of the guard standing at the foot of the steps, just as Pincher Martin launched himself feet first onto the unsuspecting guard below, a drop of about fifteen feet. At the very moment,

Geordie Day came running across the courtyard from the far side. The Irishman on guard was completely confused; someone had suddenly materialised to his right, whilst someone else was running towards him, both spelt danger!

At that precise moment, the door to the Penchester Room was opened from the inside and a second MP stepped out. Seeing the running marine, he shouted a warning, then opened fire, two quick bursts. Then he immediately dashed back into the room, slamming the door behind him. Geordie Day sprinting across the courtyard saw Dacre emerge from the shadows just as Pincher Martin jumped off the roof. As the MP on the top of the steps opened fire, Day dived sideways as the first bullet took him in his right shoulder and the second tore into his thigh. He went down and stayed down, winded and in shock, but as yet not in any pain.

Pincher Martin landed on the guard, who collapsed completely unconscious. Martin rolled to his feet, just as Dacre sprinted to Day's side and had begun to apply a field dressing in an effort to staunch the flow of blood from the leg. By this time, Martin had climbed up the short flight of steps to try the door. As he suspected, the old oak door was locked and bolted. Brum Preece up on the Gate Tower and Timber Woods on the battlements hearing the muted gunfire had both made their way down to the courtyard and were helping Dacre move the injured marine to the relative safety of a nearby wall. Martin bounded back down the steps.

"That door is well and truly locked, we'll never shift the bastards out of there!" He said. Geordie Day, who was by now in a great deal of pain, reached into an inside pocket of his combat jacket and pulled out a small pat of what looked like putty.

"Here, AJ, use this. It's a small souvenir from the old days, there is also a detonator. It should do the trick!" With that his eyes glazed over as he lapsed into unconsciousness.

Dacre took the plastic explosive and the detonator and climbed the steps to the Penchester Room two at a time. Here he fixed them to the heavy wooden door, then shouted to the others to take cover. With that, he set the detonator and then ran and jumped the six feet over the side wall of the steps to get out of the way of the blast. Three seconds later an almighty explosion shook the castle to its very foundations as the door completely disintegrated in a cloud of dense smoke. Dacre AJ was on his feet immediately.

"Come on, Pincher, let's go!"

Both marines charged up the steps through the broken door and into the room, weapons at the ready. At first, it was difficult to see anything because of the dust and smoke everywhere. Stepping over a body by the door, which was shredded to pieces and studded with splinters, rather like a hedgehog the two marines gazed in disbelief at the state of the room. It was a total shambles, furniture overturned and smashed. Lying face down in the hearth was a second body, part of this man's clothing was smouldering in the ashes of the fire. The young prince was still strapped in his chair, which was overturned and leaning drunkenly against a wall. He was bruised and battered, but otherwise alive. Dacre immediately set about releasing him. Meanwhile, Pincher Martin was checking the body in the fireplace.

"This one's still alive, AJ, shall I finish him off?"

"No! Let's not descend to their level. Just drag him out of the fireplace, he'll be no trouble to us. We'll let the police sort him out."

Dacre AJ glanced over, as the Irishman was pulled clear, the man's face looked vaguely familiar, but for the moment he couldn't place it.

Back in the courtyard Dacre, Martin and the prince were met by the others. Art Fagin had discovered the prisoners and released them and, although they were a bit shocked, they were otherwise unhurt. The marine driver, although alive, was clearly in the need of urgent medical treatment for his head wound. Dacre checked his watch, it was 01.30 hours. Timber Woods had set up the radio and was urgently calling in.

"Hello, Sunray, this is G for George, are you receiving me? Over." The sound of the loud static hiss could be heard all around the castle courtyard.

"It's no go, AJ, not a bloody thing!"

"Okay, give it another five minutes, then if you're still not through we'll have to use the verey pistol. In the meantime, let's get everyone in the kitchen and organise a hot drink. We have some decisions to make and quickly. Hot sweet tea was soon made and passed around, even Geordie Day and the driver were able to take a few sips. Dacre looked around at his somewhat battered team.

"Okay, everyone, this is the situation as I see it. Firstly, the phones are down as we expected. Secondly, we haven't been able to make contact on the radio. Thirdly, we have three injured marines who can't make it out of here by boat, and lastly, we still have to get the prince away to safety. So I propose we leave Art here in charge with Geordie and the driver. You give us a head start, say thirty minutes and then fire the green flare. That will tell those outside that we are safely away with the prince and they can stop the Sultan from coming. Of course it will also alert any IRA back-up teams in the area, but we must risk that. Our priority must be to get the prince away and the injured to hospital. Any questions or other ideas?" No one disagreed or had an alternative plan.

"Right then, let's get moving, we'll go back the way we came, over the wall." Looking at the prince, Dacre added.

"You okay with that, Sir?" The prince looked down at what was left of his little finger, still roughly bandaged.

"Yes, I'll manage, thank you. I've already had some morphine so I can't feel much anyway. Brother Cedric who had been listening to all this with a look of awe on his face suddenly interrupted Dacre.

"There is a small door from the kitchen into the garden. If you use that you won't have to climb down the outside wall, also it is possible to go around the moat by making a wide detour through the gardens. Will that be of help?"

"Thank you, Brother, that will do us nicely!"

# 28

THE last thing that Padraig O'Regan remembered was Seamus shouting that they had company as he slammed and bolted the door. The next second the whole world seemed to disintegrate into one large ball of flame, smoke and debris flying everywhere. He felt himself picked up and thrown sideways by the blast. He vaguely heard voices nearby and felt himself being dragged a short distance, but then he lapsed into the blessed relief of unconsciousness. Maybe ten minutes had passed before he came around. Propping himself up on an elbow, dazed and with the sleeve of his jacket still smouldering, he looked around. He rolled onto his knees and tried to stand, he was dizzy and felt sick. The room was a total wreck, the prince had gone and his friend's body was virtually unrecognisable; what a bloody mess, he thought to himself. He had certainly underestimated things, this whole attack looked very military, maybe even special forces. Perhaps the marines had got involved, but if so how and more importantly who? He needed a telephone. How he wished he had not cut the wires to the castle. Still with a little bit of help and a lot of luck he might be able to yet retrieve the situation.

Stepping through what was left of the door, he checked all was clear. Gingerly, he made his way down the short flight of steps into the courtyard. One of his men, he couldn't recall his name was lying in a crumpled heap. He checked for a pulse, it was there but very faint. He would have to leave him. Moving through a narrow passage, Padraig entered the inner courtyard and made his way to a postern gate set in the outer wall. He paused and tried his walkie-talkie, desperate to make contact with the boat waiting upstream. No reply! Padraig cursed! Leaving the castle, he made his way through the kitchen garden and over what was left of the old boundary wall. He continued on, passed the remains of the Norman mound, where he eventually reached the riverbank. He tried his radio, success, 'be with you in ten minutes', came the reply. Making himself comfortable on a nearby tree stump, he settled down to wait and think. The sound of a boat engine startled him. This couldn't be his boat, he reasoned, it was far too soon, so it could only be the prince's rescue team leaving. Unfortunately, he couldn't see them because of a bend in the river, but sound carries at night especially over water. He could just make out urgent whispered voices and the sound of men boarding a boat and setting off. A few minutes later, his own boat arrived with Donal Collins at the helm.

"Change of plans, Donal, we're going downstream, but keep well back, there's another boat up ahead and I don't want them to see us."


The lights at the lock allowed the Irishman to see a little more clearly what was going on. The boat ahead had pulled into the riverbank and several men had got off and headed for a parked car. Padraig reached for his radio.

"Pat? There's a car coming your way, large and black with two occupants. What? No, I don't have the fucking registration number! How many cars will there be on the road at this time in the morning?" He paused to check his watch. "Get some of your lads to follow it and stop it at all costs, do you understand, at all costs!"

# 29

Marine Tubby Taylor looked on anxiously, as Dacre AJ and the others climbed on board the Sea Cadet cutter.

"Where are Geordie and Art?" he asked.

"We've had to leave them behind, they'll be okay," replied Dacre tersely. He looked the boat over.

"Is this the best you could do?" For a split second Taylor suddenly felt unappreciated.

"Don't you worry, AJ, I've got something really special lined up down at the lock." Dacre looked at him questioningly.

Dacre AJ called Pincher Martin over to him.

"How's the prince doing?"

"He's okay, his hand is bloody sore and swollen, but he's not complaining. He's a tough little bugger I can tell you."

"Good! Look, I've decided to split our group up. I want you and Timber to take the car that the police have left and drive out of Maidstone to Canterbury and then on to Deal. I suggest you use the A20. It will be a risky business acting as a decoy, but it might buy us some extra time." Martin thought about this briefly.

"Are you sure you want to do this? You of all people will know it's not good tactics to split your force in two."

"Yes, I know. But in the circumstance I don't think we have any choice. If we split up, the Irish will have to do the same. I think it may actually help us even the odds."

"Okay, AJ, if you are really sure then, we'll give it a go." Dacre then spent the next few minutes giving Martin a very brief summary of the possibilities of how he might get the Prince back to The Depot at Deal.

"When you get back to barracks make sure you report direct to the RSM, he'll know what to do." With that, the two marines shook hands.

"We'll see you all back at The Depot then," said Martin as he and Timber Woods climbed out of the boat onto the riverbank. They then made their way across the car park to the vehicle that had been left for them.

With the two marines ashore and on their way and the canoes safely tied up on the riverbank, Taylor helmed the cutter into the open lock.

"I suggest we leave the gates open, it may look as if we haven't used the lock at all. I've another boat ready below, it's a bit faster than this old tub," he said. The small group climbed up onto the lock side and then walked quickly to the far end and down onto a floating pontoon, where a sleek thirty-five-foot cabin cruiser was tied up. Dacre was so surprised at the sight of the boat that he let out a 'well, I'll be damned.'

"What's up, AJ?"

"Nothing! The boat is fine, couldn't be better, I'll explain later." With everyone safely on board, they cast off. Dacre took the helm. He checked his watch.

"High tide was at 0100 hours, so it's well on the turn. That should give us a couple more knots of speed. We could be at Chatham in about an hour, although the sandbanks in this part of the river can be tricky. Tubby, check out down below, you should find some charts, try the right-hand cupboard on the port side. Brum, see if you can rustle up a brew for us all." The two marines went below. Dacre turned to the prince.

"You alright, Sir?" he asked.

"Yes, I'm fine, and I want to thank you for what you have done!"

"Well, we haven't finished yet, so with all due respect to your highness I suggest you save your thanks until later." With that, the marine opened the throttle so that the boat leapt forward, pushing out a large white phosphorescent wave that lapped noisily onto the riverbanks.

Back in the castle courtyard, Marine Arthur Fagin checked his watch. He then loaded and cocked the verey pistol. Pointing it to the night sky, he pulled the trigger. From the London Road, maybe a mile away, a policeman on duty saw the green flare light up the sky. He immediately put through a call to the Chief Constable, who in turn telephoned the Commanding Officer at The Depot with the news that the prince had been rescued. Shortly afterwards, Brigadier Ellis contacted General Moulton at Whitehall to inform him that the first part of the recue had been a success.

# 30

THE black Wolsey car drove slowly towards Maidstone town centre, down past the old cavalry barracks and County Hall, then along Week Street, where the occasional street light showed silent and deserted shops. It had just started to rain; the road and pavements glistened in the wet and the traffic lights seemed to shine extra brightly. The two marines sat quietly, anxious to be on their way. As the lights changed to green, Pincher Martin accelerated smoothly away, turning left into King's Street. Neither marine had noticed another car about a hundred yards behind them.

Passing the entrance to Leeds Castle, Martin did an expert but unnecessary racing change as their speed increased. The villages of Harrietsham and Lenham flew past as the road straightened. Timber Woods sitting in the passenger seat rubbed the back of his neck. He had that strange sensation which had served him well in the past. Suddenly, he felt compelled to turn around. A very bright pair of car headlights were just behind them.

"We're being followed, can't you go any faster?" he said.

"I'm already doing sixty and this old crate won't do much more," replied Martin.

At that moment, the rear window disintegrated as a hail of bullets swept the back of their car. Woods immediately heaved himself into the backseat, cocked his submachine gun and let fly an entire magazine.

"That should give the bastards something to think about!" The car behind had dropped back and was swerving from side to side, making it a difficult target. Woods expertly changed magazines.

As the fork in the road at Charing approached, Pincher Martin left it until the very last moment before he wrenched the steering wheel round into the tight left-hand turn. Tyres squealing, the car swerved onto the Canterbury Road and then up the long steep hill ahead. The car behind was far too close and therefore too late to make the same turn. It overshot the corner and skidded to a halt. With its exhaust growling softly, the Irish car turned left into Charing village and, having crossed the Pilgrim's Way, rejoined the main road to Canterbury. Valuable time had been lost; the two Irishmen were just in time to see the rear lights of the car ahead disappear around the hairpin bend at Stockers Head. Accelerating down the straight stretch of road past Chilham Castle, the two marines in their car sped through the outskirts of Canterbury. They were now closely followed by the Irish, who had managed to catch up in their more powerful car. Racing around the old city wall, both cars ignored the traffic lights as they drove past the prison and on and up St Martin's Hill into the countryside.

"We are never going to outrun them," shouted Martin. "I'm going to let them try and overtake us, then run them off the road. Get ready!" Just as they passed Littlebourne, there was a mile or so of road which was ideal. Martin decreased his speed slightly allowing the other car to come alongside them ready to overtake. Woods fired several quick bursts just as Martin flicked his steering wheel to the right. There was a harsh scrapping and tearing of metal as the two vehicles touched. The marine held his course and his nerve, a grim look on his face determined not to give way. Too late the Irishmen realised what was happening. Their car was forced off the road, up and over a grass verge and through a hedge, somersaulting into an orchard and out of site. Martin expertly corrected his tail skid and brought the car to a halt. Checking his rear view mirror he slowly reversed back up the road. Both marines stepped out of the car, weapons at the ready. They walked cautiously back up the road to the site of the crash, covering each other as they went. There was no sound except for their boots crunching on the broken glass that littered the road. The night was amazingly still. There were deep furrows on the grassy bank and the smell of petrol and burnt rubber hung in the air. The car of their adversaries lay upside down, steam was escaping from a shattered radiator, the heat from the engine ticked and crackled, one wheel was still spinning slowly. The two marines stepped through the torn hedge, down into the orchard. Using torches they had found in the glove compartment of their car they began to check the crashed car. The driver was still in his seat, the column of the steering wheel pining him to the back like a lance, his face a deathly white, grinning in a grim rictus of death. Timber Woods, who had wandered off, called out softly that he had found the passenger. The body of the Irishman was about twenty feet away, hanging upside down from the branches of a tree. Like some bizarre puppet.

"Come on, chum," said Pincher quietly." Let's get the hell out of here, we'll leave this lot for the local plod to sort out."

Ten minutes later, as they drove into Wingham, Martin said, "I'm going to take the back road, you okay with that?"

"Whatever! Just get us back to The Depot in one piece." Then, as an afterthought he added, "I never thought I would be so glad to see that bloody place again!"

# 31

THE sleek motor launch moved quickly down the river, its speed greatly assisted by the outgoing tide. Past the Friary at Aylesford, then the paper mills at New Hythe and Snodland. Then, under the new motorway bridge and into the Rochester Basin, where Short's seaplanes had once graced the water. Tubby Taylor was by now back in the wheelhouse clasping several charts in his hands.

"How did you know where to find these, AJ?" Dacre pointed to a small brass plaque screwed to the bulkhead, it read: *Dunkirk Small Boats Association.* Taylor looked at him with a puzzled frown on his face.

"Back in 1940, I was too young to go to France with my company. We were based at Chatham at the time. So instead I volunteered to help with the evacuation of troops off the beaches by the dozens of small boats. This was the boat I was on. Mr Thomas the owner and myself brought the boat down to Ramsgate from the River Medway. We did about five trips to Dunkirk. Talk about bloody chaos!"

"Is that where you got the Legion de Honour?"

"Yeh! I pulled some French general out of the water, saved him from drowning, he gave me his medal in gratitude. Their lordships at the Admiralty decided I should be allowed to keep it. All good for moral I suppose in what was a desperate time for England."

"What happened to the owner of the boat?"

"He was in film processing I think, anyway a reserved occupation. We kept in touch right up until he died in 1953, something to do with the great smog that year." Both marines lapsed into a gentle and friendly silence.

The launch continued to follow the river out to the sea, through Limehouse and the Chatham Reach and then on past the

Naval Base. The going was easier now, the channel was well marked with buoys so that warships could come and go at any hour of the day or night. Dacre checked his watch, it was 0330 hours; they had made good time. The lights of Queenborough on their starboard side were shortly followed by those of Sheerness. As they rounded Garrison Point into the Thames Estuary, the marine took particular care to avoid a sunken World War II munitions ship, whose two masts could still be clearly seen. In 1941, the American ship SS Montgomery had gone to the bottom with its cargo of explosives, bombs and fuses. Although the explosives had so far proved to be stable, the ship was a constant danger to other shipping despite warning signs and buoys. Once in the open sea, Dacre set a course of East South East, which broadly followed the coastline to Warden Point and then into Shell Ness where the Swale flows into Whitstable Bay.


Marines Taylor and Preece were scanning the seascape with the boat's powerful binoculars. The prince was below, asleep in the cabin, exhaustion having overtaken his desire not to be a burden.

"There's a boat up ahead, AJ. I can just make out her riding light, about half a mile away, looks like a motor sailor at anchor." Dacre smiled to himself, this was just where the boat, his boat should be. It was beautiful thirty-eight-foot Colvic Watson, powered by a 150hp Sea Panther engine. In good weather conditions it was quite capable of doing 16 knots and, with a good tide and the wind behind, maybe as much as 20 knots. The marines dropped a couple of fenders over the side, as Dacre skilfully brought the launch alongside the other boat. The name *ILONA Whitstable* was just visible on the stern. The two boats were quickly made fast as Dacre climbed aboard to greet his old friend Dick Browning, who was grinning from ear to ear.

"AJ, you old bugger! What brings you to this neck of the woods?" They shook hands, then the marine gave his friend a quick rundown of events, who listened carefully taking it all in.

"Okay, I've got the picture! We can't hang about here. So I suggest you take *Ilona* up to Tankerton and go ashore there to your place. Remember it's low tide, so watch out for Shingle Street. You'll have to anchor a way out and then walk in through the shallows, it should be firm enough. I'll take your borrowed launch and run it into the inlet at Seasalter near the Blue Anchor pub. It's just navigable. I can walk back to town from there and later see that the launch gets back to its owners. Anyone following you might think you have gone ashore there."

"Sounds good to me, let's get going!"

With a brief wave from the marines, the two boats cast off. Dacre AJ now at the familiar controls of his own boat set off eastwards across the Tankerton Bay. Although it was only about three miles as the crow flies, he steered slightly out to sea past the entrance to the harbour and gave the shingle bank known locally as the 'Street' a wide birth. The lights along the seafront were easily visible from the boat and, although dawn was still some way off, the sky was beginning to lighten in the east. As they moved parallel to the shore, Dacre began to count off the landmarks that he knew so well. The Continental Hotel up on the hill by the flag staff, then the Marine Hotel and the tennis courts, then the Royal Hotel and lastly the tea rooms at the Priest and Sow corner. At this point, he turned the boat in towards the shore. Carefully watching the depth gauge, he moved the boat slowly forward until he felt the keel nudge the soft sandy sea bed below. They were about a quarter of a mile from the beach.

"Right, we'll anchor here and walk in. Collect all your gear, Brum bring the Bren gun, will you." Preece and Taylor looked at each other and grinned.

"Here we go again, Per Mare Per Terram. Into the ogin once more!" The young prince looked totally perplexed. Dacre smiled.

"Don't you worry, Sir. It's our corps motto, it means By Sea By Land." Brum Preece was the first over the side, the water coming up to his chest. Holding his weapon above his head, he called out softly, "Come on in, boys, it's lovely."

The four men waded slowly ashore until they arrived at the vast expanse of mud that was only exposed at low tide. Spreading out, they sprinted across the four hundred yards or so of the ridged mudflats until they reached the steeply shelving pebble beach at the foot of the cliffs, where they threw themselves down breathing heavily.

"Wait here, I'll do a quick recce." With that, Dacre scrambled up the crumbling cliffs to the top. In front of him were the remains of a field, which as a boy he could remember being ploughed by a local farmer, now most of it had slipped into the sea. Beyond the field was an unmade road full of bumps and potholes and then a small group of semi-detached houses, one of which he had inherited from his grandfather. He cautiously looked both ways. Then using his binoculars he focussed up the track to the main road and the Priest and Sow corner. The little grocer's shop was clearly visible, as was the old teashop with the word TEAS painted in huge letters on the roof. A large black car was parked alongside the telephone box.

Apart from a small row of houses behind the stores, there were only five homes in the road itself, of which only two were permanently occupied, the others being for holidays. These were his next-door neighbours, the Miss Grahams, and further up the road the old sea captain.

Coming down the track with milk bottles clanking away, pushing her ancient milk cart was Dora from the nearby Bartletts Farm, making her early morning deliveries. Dacre checked on the parked car once more. Then keeping as low as he could, he leopard crawled across the field to the chestnut paling fence that edged the unmade road. He waited for Dora to arrive.

"Psst! Dora, it's me, AJ. Don't look this way!" Dora was so surprised that she actually jumped, but managed with the greatest of efforts not to look in his direction. Instead, she rested her cart and began to check her clipboard.

"Eh, Master AJ, you did give me a turn." This was said in her broad Kentish accent. AJ looked up the road.

"How many men in that car up by the shop?"

"Three that I could see and one in the phone box. I heard them talking, they are Irish you know."

"Thanks Dora, good girl. Now carry on delivering and whatever you do don't look back. When you get down to the last house, stop and count slowly to one hundred." Dora went to answer, but the marine was already snaking his way back across the field and then down the cliffs to the others.

"Okay, lads, it would seem the Irish are already here, well at least at the top of the road. So, we'll have to make a little detour and go into my place by the back door. Right, follow me!" With that, Dacre was off, sprinting across the shingle beach and jumping each of the wooden groynes that stretched down the beach and into the sea. With a wave of his hand, he changed direction and was scrambling up the cliffs. The others followed as best they could. At the top, he paused for a quick look-see. With a whispered 'keep as low as you can', he crawled across the grassy field to the old fence. He paused to allow the others to catch up. Dora with her milk cart was standing nearby carefully checking her deliveries.

"Right, we cross in an extended line using her as cover, everyone ready?" As one, the four men stood up and walked quickly across the road and into some tall grass and out of site. From a distance, Dacre hoped that it might just look like one person crossing, well at least that was the theory. Moving quickly with the marine in the lead, the four men made their way to a narrow grass lane at the rear of the houses and their gardens. They zig-zagged up the lane, covering each other as they went until they reached the back gate to his house. Taking it in turn, they sprinted across a well-kept lawn to the safety of the back wall of the garage. Dacre peered around the corner, checking the property, all seemed quiet. Then, with his weapon cocked and ready, he walked cautiously to the back door, which he opened with his key. Turning to the other he signalled them to come on in, which they did at a run.

# 32

With their boat barely underway, the two Irishmen cautiously approached Allington Lock. Donal spoke in a stage whisper.

"They have left the lock gates open, maybe hoping we'll think they have gone by car." Padraig nodded a reply.

"Drop me over there by the car park, I need to use the phone box. By the time I've finished you should be through the lock." As he jumped ashore, he noticed the three canoes pulled up on the riverbank. Marine Commandos, he thought. No wonder the raid had been so successful. But where had they come from? Once inside the telephone box, he dialled a number. Seconds later, a very sleepy female voice answered.

"Hello? Hello? Who is this? Do you know what the time is? Is that you Alex?"

"No, it's not bloody Alex! It's your cousin!" There was a very sharp intake of breath.

"Oh my God! You bastard! You promised me you would never contact me again!"

"I know I promised, but this is vital for the cause. Lives might depend on it, certainly mine, and you are family, so shut up and listen!" He spoke for a further five minutes, listened to the reply then hung up. Then he dialled a second number.

"Pat, it's me. Listen, there has been a change of plan. I'm pretty sure it was the marines after all who rescued the prince. The car your lads are chasing is just a decoy, can you get them back? No! Okay, we'll have to leave them. The marines have the prince on a boat going down the Medway. Donal and I are going to follow them. I now have information that suggests they are heading for Whitstable, one of them has a house near there and possibly a car. Meet me at the harbour, I'll be about three hours."

"Okay, Padraig. What about Seamus and the lads who went with you to the castle?"

"No, they are all out of it!" Pat paused before answering; after all, five men down out of six was a huge setback.

"There's only me left here now. I'll see if I can round up a couple more boys. Donal has a cousin in Whitstable, I'll try him first."

"Right, Pat. With a little bit of luck we might be able to save this project and our necks, I'll see you later." Padraig rejoined Donal on the boat.

"Bloody hell, this water is low, is the tide going out?"

"Yeh! We'll have to watch the sandbanks and in the dark that won't be easy."

"How far ahead is the other boat?" asked Donal. Padraig checked his watch.

"Maybe thirty minutes or so."

"Can we use the roof searchlight then? It would help."

"Go ahead, we need to make up as much time as we can." The trip down the river was uneventful and they did make good time. Padraig spent much of it studying an AA road map that he had found amongst all the charts and papers down below in the cabin.


If he was to retrieve the situation, he would need to plan carefully. The information he had got from his cousin about the house near Whitstable had been a great help. However, the fact that the rescue team was led by perhaps the most famous marine in the Corps of Royal Marines didn't help one little bit. Padraig thought back twenty years, when he along with hundreds of other Irishmen had chosen to enlist in the British army to fight the Nazi menace. He had actually served his time as a commando in the Royal Marines in 1941, seeing action at Dieppe and later at Normandy. It was in 48 Commando RM that he had really got to know Dacre AJ, actually being a member of his troop. Dacre was then an acting sergeant, later promoted to temporary captain since all of the officers were either dead or severely wounded. Along with everyone else in the troop, Padraig would have followed Captain Dacre to the ends of the earth, such was the undying loyalty that he had somehow inspired in his battle-hardened men. With the cessation of hostilities in 1945, Padarig left HM Forces and returned to Ireland. Sometime later, he heard on the grapevine that Dacre had chosen to revert to the rank of marine. Ironically, Padraig's meteoric rise in the IRA and his command of several ASUs was largely due to his training as a marine, which even in wartime was second to none. Few men in the Provisional IRA had his ability to organise and lead men so successfully. And now he was up against his former fellow marine and Troop Commander. This was not going to be easy, not easy at all!

Donal broke into Padraig's thoughts.

"We're just coming into Whitstable Bay. Over on your right you can just make out buildings on the shoreline." Padraig scanned the area with some binoculars.

"Looks like a pub or an inn of some sorts. Just to the left is a small creek with a launch tied up alongside."

"Do you want me to go in? It will be shallow because the tide hasn't turned yet."

"No! Let's push on to the harbour. Pat will be waiting for us, hopefully with some re-enforcements." Twenty minutes later, Donal eased their boat into Whitstable Harbour. As harbours went, it was quite small and had seen better days. There was still a dozen or more fishing boats of varying sizes tied up and resting on the mud. Some were still used for collecting oysters, for which the town had once been famous. Now like everything else to do with the harbour, the oyster beds were run down and neglected. Lying alongside the main wharf was an inshore coastal steamer, getting ready to unload its cargo of Norwegian timber. Although it was still low tide, Donal found it was just possible to get their boat alongside the cargo boat. Pat was standing on the deck looking down at them. He waved towards a rope ladder that was hanging over the side. Within minutes, the three men were reunited. Moving quickly, they crossed the deck of the steamer onto the quayside and into a waiting car. Donal's cousin Frank O'Connor was at the wheel, whilst in the back seat sat seventeen-year-old Michael O'Dwyer, better known as Mickey. The two cousins greeted each other with huge smiles and slaps on the back.

"Alright, alright, enough of the family reunion. Let's get moving! Do you know where we are going?" snapped Padraig.

"Yes, Sir, I do. I know the area very well."

"Well, what are you waiting for?" With that, Frank crunched the car into first gear and kangarooed out of the harbour car park. Padraig looked questioningly at his friend Pat.

"Don't worry, he'll be alright, he's just a bit nervous. This is his first big job. Besides, I couldn't get anyone else at such short notice." Padraig then seemed to notice Mickey for the first time, sitting sandwiched between the two big Irishmen on the back seat. Padraig sighed to himself and raised his eyes to heaven; beggars can't be choosers he supposed. Young Mickey was quiet and overawed, and just a little bit frightened. His mother would skin him alive if she ever found out what he was up to. He had gladly gone along with his friend Frank who had promised him fifty pounds in cash for a day's work. That was a lot of money to a seventeen-year-old like him. Nevertheless, he was keen to prove himself worthy, given half a chance.

Leaving the harbour, the car turned left onto the main road and crossed over the old railway line that was once the 'Winkle' line to Canterbury. Taking the coast road, they passed what looked like a castle on their right and then over the brow of the hill and down towards the grassy slopes of Tankerton sea front. Padraig was so deep in thought that he only heard snatches of Frank chattering on like a tour guide.

"in 1893 the town was first laid out...........The pier was demolished in 1913............................The hotel was used as a hospital during the Great War..........................Most houses were built between the wars............................The floods of 1952 did great damage..............................Tankerton is to Whitstable as Hove is to Brighton."

At the end of the sea front, the car turned left and stopped outside an old-fashioned teashop. Frank turned around.

"This is the Priest and Sow corner. The unmade road is Marine Crescent where your man has his place. These houses don't have numbers, only names. What is the name of his house?" Padraig looked up sharply.

"What?"

"Do you know the name of his house?" Frank repeated. Padraig thought for a minute or two, racking his brains for an answer. He did not know and he said so.

"Well, we need to know the name in order to find the right house!" Padraig felt his temper rising with this young man who was still wet behind the ears, yet he knew he was right. Angrily, he threw open the car door and got out.

"Well, then, I'll just have to get the fucking name, won't I!" With that, he stomped off towards a nearby telephone box. His cousin was going to love him! The three men sat in silence in the car, each considering their leader's outburst. The silence was rudely interrupted by a woman pushing a heavy milk cart suddenly coming into view. The clanking of the bottles sounded amazingly loud at that time in the morning.

"Shall I stop her?" asked Frank looking at his cousin. Donal turned to the back seat.

"What do you think, Pat?"

"I could do it," said Mickey speaking for the first time.

"No, let her go. She won't know anything. Besides, she's just arrived like us. Anyway, we don't want any of the locals getting twitchy and nosey because their morning milk hasn't turned up, do we? Leave her be."

# 33

THE four men stood silently in Dacre's small kitchen, steam rising from their wet clothing, the adrenalin still pumping through their veins, the events of the past few hours catching up on them. If there can be a collective feeling of exhaustion, this was it. Dacre AJ with his years of experience was the first to snap out of it, having recognised the danger signs of creeping lethargy, which was always guaranteed to lower moral and create weakness.

"Okay, lads, let's get this wet gear off. Stow your kit in your packs, then towel yourselves down while I find you some dry clothes. Then clean and check weapons whilst I rustle up some food and a hot drink. After that, I suggest you try and get some sleep. Keep the curtains closed and the lights off." Discipline took over as the men began to sort themselves out.

After a welcome scratch meal of soup, cracker biscuits and tinned sardines, washed down with hot sweet tea, liberally laced with a large tot of whiskey, the two marines and the prince had fallen asleep in the armchairs in the front room. The bandage on the young man's hand had been redressed and he seemed to be in remarkably good spirits, but maybe it was just the alcohol working its own magic. The house was still and very quiet. It smelt of polish and lavender, a sure sign that his neighbours the Miss Grahams had been around looking after the place. Dacre sipped the last of his cold tea, finalising his plans in his own mind. He got up quickly and cleared away the plates and mugs, stacking them in the kitchen sink. He suddenly felt his age. No longer a young man, he ached from head to foot. His body was trying to tell him something, he knew he was getting too old for this sort of thing. He shrugged his shoulders, he couldn't be doing with this, there were things he had to do.

Quietly he let himself out of the back door and walked the few steps to his garage. He pulled open one of the large green garage doors and stepped inside and paused on the threshold to allow his eyes to adjust to the gloomy interior. Happy memories came flooding back to him, especially of his grandfather and his family and friends sitting around a long trestle table playing cards on a Sunday afternoon, come rain or shine. The scores from their many games could still be seen pencilled onto the pale bricks of the garage wall. High up among the rafters hung a dozen or so old chairs, once painted orange, now covered in dust and cobwebs. This little semi-detached house that his grandfather had left him, had once been the family seaside holiday home. Each Saturday evening, after business had finished for the day, they would motor down in their chauffeur-driven cars in order to spend the Sunday by the sea. They would relax, eat and drink and, if the weather was warm enough, swim in the sea, and of course they would play endless games of cards. Late Sunday evening, they would be driven back to London, refreshed and ready for business on Monday morning. Dacre also remembered the time he spent here just after his grandfather died, building an old-style clinker sailing boat. It had been a form of therapy he supposed, especially with the hours of meticulous and painstaking carpentry, so that every piece fitted together with mathematical precision. Since he had never known either of his parents, it had fallen to his grandfather to bring him up. He had missed him terribly. His lovely next-door neighbours had fretted and fussed about his adolescent welfare, by keeping him well supplied with food and hot soup. Somehow he had got through his grieving and had emerged a better person. Enough of this, he thought, he couldn't be doing with it right now. He had a job to finish and finish it he would, come what may, because a Royal Marine never gives up, no matter what the odds are.

Under a heavy tarpaulin, the shape of a car was just discernible. Pulling the cover to one side revealed a Morris Minor convertible, blue with a green top. Dacre checked the oil and water and that the starting handle was in place. Satisfied that all was well, he returned to the house. From the storm porch on the front of his home, he checked that the road was clear. In three steps, he was out of the front door and had snatched the house name board from the lawn and was back inside, unseen by anyone. Moving quickly, he returned to the back garden and, still holding the name board, expertly vaulted over the dividing fence into his neighbour's garden. He gently knocked three times on their back door and let himself in. The Miss Grahams, Lil and Sue, were both in their late seventies. Sue was small and birdlike, frail-looking with short white bobbed hair. Lillian or Lil as she liked to be known was by contrast bigger and rounder than her sister, her long grey hair plaited and tied up in a bun. Both sisters had been retired since 1946. During the war, Sue had worked at Bletchley Park and still did the Times crossword every day in under fifteen minutes. Lil had done something in the Special Operations Executive, but she never talked about it. Despite their ages, both ladies were fit and well. They swam almost every day of the year and thought nothing of walking into the nearby town to do their shopping, although as they were the first to admit, they would catch a bus back. To the marine, they seemed to be ageless and he loved them like his own.

Sue was the soft one. Standing on tip-toes she reached up and threw her arms around him and whispered a welcome.

"Hello Alan John, my lovely bootneck." She was the only person ever to call him by his given name. Lil was a bit more abrupt like, yet still pleased to see the lad as she called him.

"Now then Sue put him down girl!" she said. Looking Dacre squarely in the face she continued,

"I saw you and your lads come in, so what can you tell us and more importantly what can we do to help?" The marine was thankful for this business-like approach, because he wasn't sure how much time he had. Quickly he sketched out the events of the last twenty four hours and then carefully went over the part of his plan that he wanted them to play. Without hesitation they both agreed.

"It will be nice to have something positive to do for once, eh Sue. Just like the old days," Lil said in her authoritative and commanding voice. Sue just blushed ever so slightly, her blue eyes twinkling mischievously. Making his excuses Dacre left and walked to the bottom of their garden where he let himself out into the back lane. Striding out, he moved quickly to the last house of the four and let himself into their back garden. It was a good job he thought that no-one ever bothered to lock their gates. Cautiously he went up to the house, all locked up until the summer and into the front garden. Making sure no-one could see him he swapped over the two name boards.

# 34

PADRAIG returned to the car, but didn't get back in. His friend wound down the window.

"My cousin needs a bit of time, she'll call back. You guys might as well get some sleep. I'll wait on the bench." He indicated a nearby seat that overlooked a grassy slope and some beach huts down below on a promenade. With that, he walked away, the collar of his coat turned up against the wind. He looked and was completely exhausted, but not defeated, not by a long shot. He sat and stared at the cold grey sea, slowly coming back in over the mud and sand, the tide had turned. Seagulls were swooping and wheeling overhead and in the distance he could just make several smudges on the horizon, which were the offshore wartime forts. It was almost tranquil. The ringing of the phone in the telephone box momentarily startled him. Quickly he walked the couple of paces and snatched up the phone. He listened carefully, just one word was spoken, '*Ravello*'. Padraig walked back to the car.

"Right then! I'm going to walk down this road and find the house. Watch for my signal." Without waiting for an answer, he walked off. The three Irishmen in the car looked at each but said nothing.

He walked slowly and purposefully down the unmade road carefully avoiding the potholes, past a row of Victorian villas at the top end, then an open space, wild and unkempt, a vacant lot. Next came a large well-kept lawn ideal for tennis in the summer and beside it a long narrow elegant house set well back from the track. The 'Captain's Cabin' was the name on the gate made from an old ship's wheel. A small blue car with its hood down was bumping slowly up the road towards him, an elderly woman was at the wheel. Padraig stepped off the road to allow her to pass. She acknowledged this with a wave of her hand. Now which house had she come from, he wondered? He quickened his pace past another vacant lot to a pair of semi-detached houses, pale bricks, green roof tiles and green paintwork. Here another elderly lady was closing some large side gates across a driveway. She looked up and smiled at him. The name board of this house said 'Red Sands' and its partner house was 'Rosedene'. He walked slowly on. The next pair of houses were older, white stucco and black woodwork. The first house was named 'Ivy House' and the second said 'Ravello'. He walked past, it looked closed up for the season, maybe the marines were sleeping. Perhaps there was a chance they could be caught off-guard? He turned and waved to the car at the top of the road. It drove down as quickly as it could to meet him.

"Right then, two teams, front and back. Patrick you and Donal take the rear entrance. Frank, you and Mickey come with me." Within seconds both doors had been forced open as the teams entered with weapons at the ready. The house was silent and empty. Patrick wiped his hand across the top of a small table, dust!

"Not been used for a while," he said. Padraig cursed!

"Frank, check upstairs, will you!" Frank clattered up the stairs with all the finesse of a cart horse.

"Nothing here, boss", he called down. Donal was checking out the garden through the back room window.

"There's a gate in the back fence, maybe they got out that way?" Padraig looked up.

"Check it out, but be discrete." Donal was there and back quickly.

"There's a grass pathway which leads up to main road." Padraig called up the stairs.

"Frank, come down here quickly!" Frank jumped down the stairs three at a time almost tripping over in the process.

"That main road, where does it go?" he asked.

"Down to Swalecliffe, then either the back road to Herne Bay or onto the by-past, the Thanet Way," said Frank.

"Where does that go?"

"Like its name says, down to the Isle of Thanet, you know Margate, Ramsgate, Broadstairs and so on."

"If I wanted to get to Deal, could I go that way?"

"Yes, I suppose you could, via Minster and Sandwich, why?" Padraig thought furiously for a minute. He felt certain they had gone that way, but how and in what? He suddenly felt very lonely.

"Come on, let's get moving, we can't do anything standing here." As they walked up the front path, something caught Padraig's eye.

"Pat, that name on the board, what do you notice?"

"Nothing! It's just a name on a wooden board stuck in the ground."

"Yes, I know that!" said Padraig impatiently. "But what colour is it?"

"Green with white letters," he replied.

"So what colour is the house?"

"What?"

"What colour is the fucking house?"

"It's black and white."

"That's right, black and white. No Brit would ever have a different colour for their name board. They just don't do that!" He snatched up the board. "Come on, we have been had!" he walked quickly back up the road.

"There, look 'Red Sands', see the board is black and white, yet the house is painted green. They have been switched! Of course damn it, the car I saw earlier, the one driven by the old lady came from here. She must have driven it around to the main road for them. That was clever, very bloody clever!"

"Shall I find the two old biddies and question them?" said Frank a little too eagerly.

"Okay, but not you. Donal, take young Mickey with you but be quick. I suggest you start next door here, it's the only house that looks lived in, and Donal if you find them take it easy, we are not here to make war on elderly women." Donal nodded to Mickey and the pair of them sprinted down the side passage of the house and around to the back door, which was under a glass covered veranda. The door was well and truly locked.

Inside the dim interior of their house, the two Miss Grahams had sat patiently waiting for nearly an hour. It had been during their early morning breakfast that Lil, ever practical, had suggested that they had better be prepared for unwanted visitors, just in case the Irish came a-calling. Sue, her blue eyes twinkling with all the excitement sat at the top of the staircase, almost in the dark. On her lap was her favourite axe which she used every morning to cut the kindling for the stove which was allowed to go out each night. Why they let it go out each night she couldn't remember, but it must have been for a good reason. She breathed slowly and evenly, and despite her age she was not in the least bit afraid. Lil sat downstairs in their little kitchen come scullery. She sat on a chair with her back to the wall out of site of the window. On her lap was her service revolver, a Webley pistol, issued to her in 1938. She had stripped, cleaned and oiled the pistol thoroughly the night before. She remembered that as a youngster she had been very good at weapon handling during the war years and had even qualified as a marksman. She had a clear view of the back door and an excellent field of fire. Despite her little heart condition, she was calm and her hands were perfectly steady.

The two Irish lads tried the back door again.

"Come on, Donal" said Mickey, "We'll put our shoulders to the door. Those two old biddies won't know what's hit them when we get inside." Donal was less sure about breaking in, especially since Padraig had told them to be quick. Mickey, however, was more than keen to prove himself and was really up for this. He stepped back a couple of paces and with his right shoulder slightly down flung himself full pelt against the centre of the door, which unable to withstand his twelve stone, splintered and gave way. In the kitchen, Lil had stood up and with her feet apart and her legs slightly bent, she held her pistol in the classic two-handed stance. The gun was cocked and ready. It was amazing, she thought, it was just like riding a bicycle, you don't ever forget your training. As the back door splintered and flew open, Mickey O'Dwyer found himself standing in the doorway, completely off balance and with the daylight behind his body, he was outlined like a target on a firing range. Without consciously taking aim, Lil fired a single shot. Whether it was by intention or accident no one will ever know, the bullet creased Mickey's scalp and embedded itself in the door frame. He let out a fearful yelp both of surprise and pain. He clapped his hands to his injured head, blood already seeping through his fingers and dripping down his face. He turned and in a blind panic bolted past his friend, ran down the garden path, climbed over the fence and was gone. This had been all too much for him. His mother would 'kill' him when he got home. Donal carefully backed away from the doorway as a voice from inside called out.

"Do you want any more boys, there's plenty left?" Discretion being the better part of valour, Donal ran back to the front of the house.

"What the hell has been going on?" demanded Padraig. Donal explained quickly.

"Do you want us to take them out?" asked Patrick.

"No for God's sake! Enough is enough! Let's get going. We know the car that the marines are in, they can only be about ten minutes ahead of us, if that. If we push ourselves we should be able to catch them up."

# 35

IT was 0500 hours by the time Marines Martin and Woods had parked their borrowed car outside the guardroom at The Depot RM. Neither marine was in a mood to be trifled with, an unscheduled stop to change a punctured tyre had not improved their sense of humour. And now to top it all, the corporal guard commander was dithering about waking the Duty SNCO, let alone the RSM. It has to be said that the corporal was extremely wary of these two marines standing in front of him. Their still partially blackened faces and the fact that they were heavily armed should have told him that they didn't want to be messed about. There was, he will admit later, a real sense of urgency about them, the atmosphere had been electric with anticipation. However, his standing orders were quite explicit, in an emergency the Duty NCO must be the first point of contact. So why wasn't he answering his phone? A more experienced corporal might have seen his way around this problem. But this young JNCO was straight from his promotion course and still lacked that certain something that only time in the Corps can bring.

The delay was unbearable! Pincher Martin was beside himself with anger, whilst Timber Woods feared that his friend might do something that later he might regret.
"Fuck this for a lark, cover my back Timber!" Martin raised his SMG, cocked it and stepped up to the guard commander's desk. Very deliberately he placed the muzzle of the weapon on the corporal's chest.
"Scrub round the Duty SNCO, get me the RSM now!" he growled. The corporal swallowed hard, he had never been threatened before. He wanted to say something, but the look in the marine's eye told him not to.

"Do it now corporal, do it fucking now!" A none too gentle prod with the SMG persuaded him to do as he was told. He dialled the RSM's number.

"Sir, I have two marines here, they say they must see you straight away. They have just arrived by car from Maidstone." The corporal listened open-mouthed to his instructions, which he repeated out loud to make sure he had got them correct.

"They are to go immediately to your office. Then I am to phone the Commanding Officer, the Second in Command and the Adjutant and I am to say *Operation Saint George,* O Group at 0700hours. Yes, Sir, that is clear." The corporal hung up the phone deeply puzzled. He went to say something to the two marines, but they were already long gone, sprinting across to the South Barracks.

The RSM was already in his office by the time the two marines arrived.

"Sit yourselves down lads, you look absolutely flakers." He reached into his desk draw and produced two glasses and his bottle of rum. Just as he was pouring them a stiff tot, the Brigadier walked in.

"Carry on, Mr McFee, don't mind me, they look as though they need a stiff drink." For the next thirty minutes or so, Martin and Woods gave a detailed 'sitrep' on the attack at Allington Castle and the release of the prince. They then talked about their eventful journey back and lastly what Dacre had in mind in order to get the prince back to safety. The Brigadier and the RSM looked at each other. The RSM spoke first.

"Alright lads, you've done very well. Now get yourselves showered and changed and then some breakfast. After that get your heads down for a bit, okay?" Both marines nodded in agreement.

"Sir, there is just one thing," said Martin. "If you are planning something, me and Marine Woods here would like to be involved, wouldn't we Timber?" Woods just smiled a reply. The RSM looked at the Brigadier who mouthed a silent yes.

"Okay lads, I'll see you get a shake, now off you go."

With the departure of the marines, the two seasoned campaigners moved into action, discussing, and formulating a plan of action.

"I'll inform Whitehall and General Moulton and clear this with the Home Secretary, if you collect the necessary maps and the details of how many trained soldiers we have available. Also you had better alert the instructor of our most senior recruit squad, I think we are going to need them. Let's hope they are up to it. We're meeting at 0700 hours?"

"Yes, Sir, your office with the Adjutant and Mr Blair."

"Good! There is just one other thing Mr McFee. The second in command has ….." he paused with some embarrassment. "He has a somewhat limited experience of combat. Perhaps it would be best if we put Martin and Woods with him, just to keep an eye on things."

"Yes, Sir. I completely understand. I'll see to it."

The clock in the Brigadier's office showed seven o'clock. Apart from the loud ticking, the room was amazingly quiet. The four men were all studying the large OS map hastily pinned up on the wall. The Brigadier coughed slightly.

"Right gentlemen to business! It now seems likely that Dacre and his team will attempt to come in via Sandwich. There are four possible routes of arrival." He pointed to the map with his cane. "Firstly here across the toll bridge, then here on this minor road to the north of the town. Then there is the Canterbury Road here and lastly this minor road in the south. These three you will notice all have level crossings. Now we have the authority from the Home Office to set up road blocks under the guise of an IS exercise. The local police will assist. I propose we take the most senior squad plus a handful of Trained Soldiers. We'll divide them into four sections of about fifteen men each. Dress of the day will be battledress rather than fatigues, since we shall be in the public eye. All ranks are to have SLR rifles and fighting orders, oh and they will need their entrenching tools. Each man is to have three full magazines and I want a Bren gun for each section. The trained soldiers are to have smoke and Mills grenades. We will also need some rolls of barbed wire and plenty of sand bags." Turning to the Adjutant, he continued,

"John, I want you to liaise with the TQMS for our supplies and ammunition." Then turning to his second in command, "Alex, talk to the MTO, we'll need four three tonners and four landrovers. Also alert the galley staff for a hot midday meal in hay boxes. Then contact the MO, I want an SBA for each section and the sickbay needs to be ready to receive any possible casualties. Mr McFee, please ask the First Drill to take the morning parade and remind him that we have our Zeebrugge Day guest arriving at 1100 hours. He had better detail some recruits to look after him. Squad instructors and training staff will have to cope with today's training programme. If all else fails, build in some make and mend time. We'll parade after breakfast at 0800 hours in front of the theatre. We should be in position by 0915 at the latest. Set up road blocks and dig in where possible, fire trenches will do and then site your Bren guns. Make sure you put trained soldiers on them. The RSM will give you further details and grid references for each of your locations. Any questions?" Both the Adjutant and the second in command raised their hands.

"John, you first."

"Sir, what about communications? Shall we take radios?"

"Good point! Draw five R42s. One for each of us and ask the Signals Officer to have the other one manned here to act as HQ. Make bloody sure you have got someone competent to act as signaller, you all know how temperamental these radios can be. The RSM will sort out call-signs. Alex, your question?"

"With us closing down these roads, what about traffic control?"

"The local police will be setting up diversions and directing traffic flow. The East Kent Bus Company has been alerted and will reroute as best they can. Remember, nothing goes out through our road blocks and stop and check everything coming in. There will be a policeman with each of you, but you are in charge not him. If there is nothing else, then I suggest we get some breakfast, it's going to be a long day."

With the office to himself, the Brigadier sat behind his desk thinking through the strategy that he and the RSM had earlier agreed. He hoped they had covered all eventualities. He was also very concerned about his second in command Major Blair. The major's unwarranted and ill-disciplined outburst the previous evening had left Brigadier Ellis with an uneasy feeling about the man's ability to command men in the field. He had considered not including him in this action, but had eventually reasoned that the major was his second in command and therefore entitled to take part. He hoped he wasn't going to be proved wrong.

# 36

THE two marines and the young prince each had a steaming hot cup of tea in front of them. They were sitting at Dacre's dining room table and despite being dog-tired and red-eyed from lack of sleep, were listening intently as he outlined his plan.

"My two neighbours from next door will take my car up to the top of the back lane, where they will park it. We'll stay in civvies and just take our weapons and spare magazines. Brum, I think the Bren gun is too big and bulky to take with us, so we had better leave it here along with our packs and other equipment. I plan to head down the bypass towards Herne Bay and then go inland. My car will be slow, especially with the four of us in it, so we'll keep to the back roads, just in case the Irish catch up with us. If there are no questions, I suggest we get going." The four of them left the house and quickly made their way up the back lane to the parked car. To the casual observer, these four men were an unusual sight, dressed as they were in an assortment of ill-fitting jeans, tracksuit trousers and pullovers. Each of them was holding his SMG under an arm in a rather futile effort to hide the weapon. Taylor and Preece had tapped several of their magazines together for speed and efficiency, in a manner not found in any weapon handling booklet. With Dacre AJ at the wheel, they drove down the road to nearby Swalecliffe, and then under the railway bridge and onto the Thanet Way. In no time at all, the little blue car was just a dot in the distance.

***

The black saloon car with the four Irishmen in it sped into Swalecliffe. Frank was at the wheel and truth be told he was enjoying this whole experience. Passing the shops on the right and the garage on the left, the car with its tyres squealing in protest, screeched under the bridge and onto the bypass, headed towards the Thanet towns.

"Put your foot down for crying out loud," shouted Padraig. "They can't be very far ahead."

\*\*\*

Dacre AJ had the accelerator pressed to the floor. Despite this, the little car was barely making forty five miles an hour. Beside him sat the prince looking pale and anxious, his hand, or more precisely the stump of his finger, was hurting like hell. Tubby Taylor leaned over from the back seat.

"Bloody hell, AJ, can't you go any faster?" Dacre gripped the steering wheel more tightly as if that would make a difference.

"No! This is the best we can do. It's the floor that is slowing us down."

"What?"

"The floor of the car is….. Never mind I'll explain later. We'll be turning off shortly." Brum Preece who had been watching the road suddenly called out,

"There's a large black car coming up fast behind us!" The little car lurched into a tight turn as they took a roundabout and headed inland towards the village of Herne.

\*\*\*

Donal half turned in his seat so that he could talk to those in the rear of the car,

"There's a small blue car up ahead, got the top down, it could be the ones we are looking for?" Patrick spoke first,

"Just follow it and whatever you do don't lose it!"

\*\*\*

The marine drove the little car into Herne, round past the church and left past the Smugglers Inn and up into the small village of Hunter's Forstal and then into Broomfield. The roads were little more than country lanes, narrow and suitable really for only one vehicle at a time. Dacre smiled grimly to himself, speed wouldn't help the Irish here. He hoped that by coming this backway he had managed to even things up a little bit. They were now on the old Roman Road, which used to connect Canterbury to Reculver on the coast; it was the only piece of straight road for miles and they had to use it, there was no choice. Luckily, it was only for a short distance.

"They're still with us," shouted Brum, the wind whipping his words away. Both he and Taylor had adopted fire positions in the back seat, their weapons at the ready, leaning on the folded down roof for support. Dacre turned off the road into Hoath and then on through the hamlet of Chislet. Within a short while, they had crossed the A28, the Margate Road, and then turned right down a short steep hill, over a level crossing and directly onto the small hand-operated 'Grove Ferry'. Thank the good Lord, thought Dacre, that the ferry is on our side of the river.

"Quick out of the car, Brum, you and Tubby close the crossing gates. Sir? Help me start cranking the ferry across." The two marines moved swiftly, slamming the gates shut. Then sprinting for all their worth they both took a running jump onto the departing ferry, which was already about four feet from the river bank. With more willing hands they were soon on the other side of the river.

"We'll tie her up here, that should slow the Irish down a bit."

"Here they come! Shall we give them a burst?" Both marines had adopted a kneeling position. Dacre looked around, the Grove Ferry pub was very close, some civvy might get injured.

"No, leave them, let's get going."

\*\*\*

The car with the Irish in it came to an abrupt halt, actually sliding into the level crossing gates. With the exception of Frank who was at the wheel, they all piled out just in time to see the marines on the other side of the river climb into their car and drive away.

"Shall I give them a burst?" asked Donal.

"No! Leave them, they're too far away. Come on, let's get these gates open, then Frank can climb across the rope and release the ferry."

"He's going to love that!"

***

From the ferry, Dacre headed eastwards, over the Little Stour River to Preston. From there he deliberately took the back lanes to Elmstone and Upper Goldstone, which led to Richborough Castle, an old Roman fort that had once guarded the Wantsum Channel. Things were going well, they were only a couple of miles from Sandwich, and from there it was only a hop and a step to Deal and safety. The only problem with driving in these back lanes was that the hedge rows were so high it was impossible to see around a corner. As they neared the castle, Dacre was momentarily distracted as he drove into a blind corner, he changed down a gear and accelerated out of the bend. He had absolutely no chance in avoiding the tractor and trailer that was blocking the lane. He did his best to stop, slamming on the brakes, but with little use. With the wheels locked, the car slid forward into the trailer with a sickening tearing crunch of metal. Dacre braced himself on the steering wheel and shouted a warning to the others, but it was too late. The prince was thrown forward, catching his head on the dashboard, rendering him semi-conscious. The two marines in the back seat were less lucky. Facing the wrong way, they had nothing to stop themselves from being catapulted over the windscreen onto the bonnet of the car and into the road. The tractor driver who was completely unhurt, stared in total disbelief at the scene of carnage in front of him. Then he saw the weapons and decided to beat a hasty retreat.

***

Whilst Donal and Frank were sorting out the ferry, Padraig and Patrick were studying a road map of the area.

"Do you think they'll go on the main roads?" asked Patrick.

"I doubt it. They know that we can catch them up, so my best guess is that they will keep to the back lanes." He traced a line from the ferry to the castle and then to Sandwich. "It's a long shot, but we have got to try it."

***

Dazed but unhurt, Dacre dragged himself out of the car. The prince was slowly coming around, he'd have a nasty bump on his head and a thundering headache, perhaps even some concussion, but other than that he seemed okay. Brum Preece was lying on the road half under the tractor, unconscious. His left arm was twisted at an unreal angle and there was a deep gash across his forehead that was bleeding so profusely that his face was covered in blood. The inside of his left leg was split from knee to crotch and blood was oozing through his trousers. Tubby Taylor was less fortunate. Although there wasn't a mark on him, the angle of his neck and his sightless eyes shouted all too loudly, broken neck. Dacre knelt down and checked for a pulse, nothing! He gently closed Tubby's eyes. He felt sickened! Fuck, what a bloody mess. By this time the prince had dragged Preece clear and was beginning to administer some first aid. Thankfully, the big marine was beginning to come around.

"Right, we can't stay here," said Dacre. "Those Irish bastards could be right up our backsides at any time. It's only about two miles to Sandwich. From there we can phone in. Brum, are you up for this?" The marine was looking at Taylor's body.

"Are we going to leave him?" he said quietly.

"We'll come back for him later, he knows that. Our first priority is to get the prince to safety."

"Okay, lead on, I'll manage."

\*\*\*

Frank eased the big car gently around the corner of the road and promptly stood on the brakes. He stared open-mouthed at the accident in front of him. The others in the car cursed his driving yet again, until they realised why he had stopped.

"This might be an ambush, so be ready," said Padraig. All four men got out of the car and advanced cautiously up the road, weapons at the ready. Patrick put his hand on the bonnet of the blue car.

"Still warm," he said. Padraig knelt by the body of the dead marine.

"So is this poor sod, so they are not very far ahead."

"There is plenty of blood around," said Donal. "So someone has been badly hurt. That should slow them down."

"Can we move the tractor out of the way?"

"No! We'll have to go on foot, but be careful. Frank, you take the lead, will you?"

\*\*\*

Within half a mile, it became clear that Brum Preece wasn't going to make it. Despite his dogged perseverance, his leg wound had reopened and he was losing a lot of blood. He was slowing the others down and he knew it.

"It's no use, AJ, you'll have to leave me here." With that, he collapsed against a field gate, his face contorted in pain. "Give me a couple of weapons so that when they come I can hold them up for a bit, that will give you a chance to get the lad here to safety." Dacre looked at the marine. Although he shook his head, he knew that Brum was right, and yes it might buy them some much needed time. Dacre looked around, the gateway had a natural view right down the lane. It was as good a place as any for a standoff.

"Okay, Brum, you're right, but I will come back for you just as soon as…"

"Forget it, AJ, just get the prince back to barracks," then with a smile,

"Go on, fuck off the pair of you, I'm expecting guests to my party and you're not invited."

\*\*\*

Frank was understandably nervous. This game of chase that they had been playing and which he had been enjoying, had suddenly become real and deadly. Moving slowly with his weapon ready, he walked down the middle of the lane, the other three were in a file behind him. Although his stomach was turning over with sickness and fear and his legs felt like rubber, he noticed how peaceful it was, even the birds were singing; it all seemed unreal. Frank never actually heard the shots fired at him. The first thing he knew or rather felt was a sledgehammer blow to his chest. He staggered back a couple of paces with the impact and looked down in amazement at the blood spurting down the front of his jacket. Slowly he sank to his knees, then like a limp rag doll, rolled forward onto his face. The birds had stopped singing!

As soon as the first shot was fired, the other three men had thrown themselves to the ground for cover. Donal was the first to move, scrambling up and over the hedge-bank and into the neighbouring field. Both Padraig and Patrick shouted to him to stop, but he didn't hear them. His cousin was lying dead and he wanted revenge. Sheer anger and blind rage drove him forward, unthinking and unprepared. He saw the marine lying at the foot of the gate, peering down the lane. Without really taking aim, he fired from the waist at least half a magazine of his submachine gun. He watched as the bullets kicked up the grass as they tore across the open ground and into the marine's legs and lower body.

\*\*\*

Brum Preece watched the four Irishmen walk slowly up the lane towards him. The leading man, not more than a boy really, was about twenty yards from his position. He checked that the fire selector switch was set on single shots rather than automatic. The 9mm Stirling submachine gun had a magazine capacity of thirty rounds. But it was the custom to load with only twenty-eight so as not to stress the magazine spring. Deadly accurate up to twenty-five yards, the weapon had been developed for house clearing and jungle fighting. It had replaced the commandos much loved sten-gun. Beyond twenty-five yards it was less effective. He had once witnessed a sergeant wearing a greatcoat that had been soaked in water over night, that had been shot at on the twenty-five yard range, only to receive nothing more than some bruises. That had been a very salutary lesson.

The marine had taken deliberate aim and had fired three single shots at the man advancing towards him. All three shots had found their target, not a difficult thing to do at that range. He saw that the other Irishmen had thrown themselves to the ground and in doing so had disappeared from his view. He eased his painful leg into a more comfortable position. Suddenly, he felt as if a giant hand had picked him up and thrown him to one side. Fighting against such pain as he never knew existed, he forced his eyes open. There, not more than ten feet away was his assailant, surveying his handiwork. Somewhere in the dim recesses of his mind, the marine suddenly remembered with amazing clarity the advice given to him by a weapons instructor years ago: 'never assume your enemy was down, always make sure, two shots to the body and one to the head.' The Irishman hadn't done that. That was his first and last mistake. With a great deal of effort, the marine managed to raise his weapon and flicking the switch to auto, fired the remainder of the magazine, some twenty-five rounds, which at that distance virtually cut the Irishman in half. With a sense of achievement at having bought some time for the others, Brum rolled over and closed his eyes.

\*\*\*

Dacre had a firm grip on the prince's collar. Both men were labouring, the prince more so, still groggy from the accident. The marine unceremoniously and with little regard for the prince's royal ancestry, half dragged the younger man along the lane in a desperate attempt to keep ahead of the Irish. The sound of gunfire from back down the road told him that they weren't very far behind.

\*\*\*

Padraig and Patrick looked across at each other. Padraig gestured for his friend to go over the hedge, whilst he went forward up the lane. With considerable caution, both men began to move. Walking slowly Padraig paused and knelt by Frank's body, feeling for any possible pulse, nothing! Patrick by this time had rolled over the hedge and was moving up the side of the field. He didn't even bother to stop and check Donal, the blood and gore and the mass of black flies already gathering spoke volumes. Further up the field he found the marine who lay in a crumbled heap against the gate. Patrick kicked away the weapon and then knelt to check for any signs of life. There was a pulse, it was very feint, but it was there.

"This one is still alive, but only just!"

"Leave him, we need to keep moving!"

\*\*\*

Major Alex Blair was nervous and on edge. His road block had been set up just beyond the level crossing gates as ordered. The marines were all in position, fire trenches had been dug on the roadside and the Bren gun had been sighted. The major was striding back and forth, constantly telling the recruits and trained soldiers to be on the alert and to be ready. The major's nervousness and lack of experience seemed to be infectious and was beginning to spread. Even the handful of experienced marines were starting to get twitchy. Marines Martin and Woods looked on with increasing concern, in their experience this did not bode well.

\*\*\*

Dacre and the prince came staggering around a corner in the lane in something akin to a slow run. Major Blair saw two men dressed in civilian clothes, both carrying weapons. He continued to stand even though his legs felt like jelly and his bowels seemed to have turned to water. He sensed a trickle of urine run down his inner thigh. Without thinking about who these two men were, he somehow forced out the command to open fire. The waiting recruits and marines needed no further bidding as a hail of small-arms fire and the heavy thud of the Bren-gun poured down the lane. Martin and Woods had, however, recognised Dacre and the prince and had leapt to their feet screaming for all their worth,
"Cease fire, cease fire! The incoming are friendly! Stop you stupid bastards, they are ours!"

\*\*\*

Dacre saw the road block and heard the command to open fire almost at the same time. With a super human effort, he managed to throw the prince into a nearby roadside ditch, before the first bullets cut him down, lifting him of his feet and dumping him down on top of the younger man.

\*\*\*

The two Irishmen sprinted around the corner just as the marines had opened fire and were met by a hail of bullets. Patrick was hit several times and, although badly wounded, he managed to return fire, in particular aiming at the one figure he could actually see, who for some reason or other was standing up. Padraig meanwhile had dived into a nearby ditch and was also returning fire. Like his friend, he tended to concentrate on the standing figure, which eventually collapsed, riddled with bullets. Padraig heard the shouted command to cease fire. He looked across at his friend and compatriot, who was by now lying very still. His eyes were open and he tried to say something, but no words came out. He just lay there mouthing the word 'go'. Padraig thought about whether or not to make one last attempt to kill the prince, but no, it would be useless. He would be cut down in seconds and anyway what purpose would it serve? His old officer had won, he had lost! Without too much effort, he managed to slide into the neighbouring field and humiliated and defeated he made his escape.

\*\*\*

Ignoring the body of the second in command, Martin and Woods sprinted up the lane to where they had seen Dacre and the prince fall into the ditch. There they found the marine, blood everywhere, lying in the arms of the young prince who was rocking him gently, like a mother rocks her child.

# EPILOGUE

The local police aided by officers from the Special Branch carried out an amazingly efficient operation in 'cleaning up' this whole business. From Allington Castle to the house in Tankerton, to the site of the accident and the scene of the final fire fight, nothing was overlooked. Even the driver of the tractor and trailer found himself signing the Official Secrets Act.

Patrick Ryan and to a lesser extent Joe Kilkenny gave invaluable information to the security forces, not only on this particular operation, but also on future planned PIRA activities on the mainland. So much so that it put the IRA's plans back by a number of years. Ryan eventually recovered from his wounds. He then spent the next thirty years being detained at Her Majesty's pleasure, much of it in solitary confinement. He was eventually released in 1992 and now lives in Donegal, Ireland, with his niece and her husband. Kilgenny is permanently confined to a wheelchair, such was the damage done to his spine when Marine Martin jumped on him. He spent twenty years in prison and now lives in Dublin.

Padraig O'Regan managed to slip away in all of the confusion. He made his way across the fields to the main road and managed to hitch a lift back to London. Several months later, his body was discovered by some neighbours at the bottom of his garden. A single shot had been fired to the back of his head. The IRA is totally unforgiving!

Marine 'Brum' Preece was found alive, but only just. He spent six months at the Royal Naval Hospital, Hasler, Portsmouth. He received a medical discharge and was also under doctor's orders never to drink again, owing to a very serious medical condition. Despite that, he now runs a pub in Southsea, opposite the main gates to the Royal Marines Barracks at Eastney.

Marine 'Pincher' Martin was reassessed for the SBS and passed with flying colours. In due course, he became the Sergeant Major (QMS) responsible for training at JSWAC in Poole, Dorset.

Marine Arthur Fagin recovered quickly from his broken collar bone. He was given his two stripes back and later made the rank of Colour Sergeant PTI at what was the ITCRM but is now the CTCRM at Lympstone in Devon.

Marine 'Geordie' Day made a full recovery. He retrained in the new specialist qualification of Royal Marines Provost. He eventually became a special duties officer and later commanded the 3rd Commando Brigade Provost Section of the Royal Marines Police.

Marine 'Timber' Woods left the Corps in September 1962 at the end of his nine-year engagement. He now runs a number of fruit and veg stalls in Deptford High Street, London, and can often be found in his favourite pie and eel shop just down the road.

Marine 'Tubby' Taylor and Major Alex Blair were both buried discretely, but with honours. In the Royal Marines chapel at Deal, a brass plaque was erected to both men.

Marine John West, the Commanding Officer's driver fully recovered from his ordeal. He did go to the 1964 Olympics, but as a reserve for the discus throwing event. He didn't actually compete.

Marine Dacre AJ made a full recovery despite the fact that he had been shot three times. He lost the middle finger of his right hand, half of his left ear was completely shot away and he was wounded in his right thigh, the bullet exiting from his backside. He survived, he said, largely because it was inexperienced recruits doing the shooting. They were understandably nervous and nervous men do not shoot straight. Today he lives quietly in Woodbridge, Suffolk, with his wife. They have four children, four grandchildren and two great children.

Dacre's car was unable to go more than 45mph because he had had the floor replaced by a well-meaning vehicle mechanic at Stonehouse Barracks RM, Plymouth. Finding himself short of the appropriate metal, the mechanic had welded in half inch armour plating, which was sufficiently strong to withstand the blast of most land mines at the time. But of course it was at the expense of a decent speed.

Petty Officer Susan Kelly left the Royal Navy the following year. During Dacre's convalescence, they struck up a lasting friendship. They eventually married on the 11th April 1964. At that time, no one knew of her family connections to Padraig O'Regan; they were second cousins.

Major General Moulton RM was successful in that he managed to convince the Joint Chiefs of Staff and Lord Mountbatten for the need to develop amphibious warfare. This resulted in two LPDs being built, later commissioned as HMS Intrepid and HMS Fearless. Indeed, much of the Royal Marines present-day capabilities are directly due to this man's continued efforts.

The young security officer at the Indonesian Embassy was quietly returned to his country, his career in the military at an end.

He served in a remote outpost on a small island just of Kai Besar for nearly forty years.

The retired and elderly Sergeant Lynch VC RM did visit The Depot RM on the 23$^{rd}$ April 1962 (Zeebrugge Day). He was looked after by recruits from the 777 Squad.

The Sultan and his son returned to Brunei. In September 1962, a rebellion backed by President Sukarno of Indonesia broke out in the Sultanate as predicted. This led to 42 Commando RM being rapidly deployed from Singapore and the 'Limbang Landing' action by' L' Company. Although the rebellion was put down by mid-1963, it heralded the period known as 'The Confrontation' in Borneo, which lasted well into the late 1960s. The Sultanate remains one of Britain's strongest allies in the Far East.

The 'Green Beret' remains the distinctive hallmark of the Royal Marines Commando. Those who wear it have gone through months of intensive and gruelling training. They will have displayed qualities of individual strength as well as teamwork and cheerfulness in adversity. A Royal Marine will not give up and will refuse to accept a situation as totally hopeless – *'it's a state of mind.'* In this respect nothing has really changed.

As befits a most secretive and sensitive mission, nothing was ever recorded in any annals or papers of the Royal Marines. The museum at Eastney has no knowledge of these events. Nothing ever appeared in any newspaper or on radio or television. No officers or men ever mentioned these events in any of their diaries or memoirs.

It was as if it never happened…!

# BIBLIOGRAPHY

Coogan, Tim Pat; *Michael Collins* Arrow Books

Edwards, KC; *Nottingham and its Region* British Association, 1966

Falconer, Barrie; *First into Action* Warner Books 1998

Ladd, James; *Royal Marine Commando* Hamlyn 1982

Lund, Paul & Ludlam Harry; *The War of the Landing Craft* NEL 1976

Neillands, Robin; *By Sea & Land* Orion Books 1987

Mercer, Peter; *Not by Strength by Guile* Blake 2001

Moulton, JL; *The Royal Marines* Sphere 1973

Parker, John; *SBS* Headline 1997

Pitt, Barrie; *Special Boat Squadron* Century 1983

Pitt, Barrie; *Zeebrugge* Four Square Books 1959

Preece, Steven; *Amongst the Marines* Mainstream 2004

Reeman, Douglas; *Knife Edge* Arrow Books 2006

Sleight, Steven; *Complete Sailing Manual* DK 1999

Thompson, Julian; *The Royal Marines* B&E 1986

White, Terry; *The SAS and Special Forces* Magpie 2004

Young, Peter; *Storm from the Sea* William Kembler 1958

# GLOSSARY

| | |
|---|---|
| ASU | Active Service Unit (IRA) |
| AWOL | Absent without leave |
| Badge | See 'Three Badger' below |
| BAOR | British Army on the Rhine |
| BCSM | Band Company Sergeant Major |
| Bootneck | Naval slang for Royal Marines |
| Bren gun | Light machine gun (.303 or 7.62 calibre) |
| Chippie | Carpenter |
| Cdo | Commando, a unit of about 600 Royal Marines |
| CO | Commanding Officer |
| Cockle | Two man canoe |
| CSM | Company Sergeant Major RM |
| DCM | Distinguished Conduct Medal |
| DQs | Detention Quarters (military prison) |
| Eating irons | Knife, fork & spoon |
| First Drill | Senior Drill Instructor RM (usually a QMS in rank) |
| Flakers | Exhausted |
| Folboat | Collapsible two man canoe |
| Galley | RN/RM term for the kitchen |
| Gash-hand | Spare person, no real job or use |
| Heads | RN/RM term for toilets, showers & washroom |
| HQ | Headquarters |
| IRA | Irish Republican Army |
| IS | Internal Security |
| ITCRM | Infantry Training Centre RM Lympstone, Devon |
| JNCO | Junior non-commissioned officer (corporal/lance corporal) |
| JSWAC | Joint Services Amphibious Centre, Poole, Dorset |

| | |
|---|---|
| King's Badge | In 1918 King George V directed that the most senior recruit Squad of the Royal Marines should be titled 'The King's Squad' and that the most outstanding recruit be awarded 'The King's Badge'. |
| LPDs | Landing Platform Docks (HMS Fearless & Intrepid) |
| LPH | Landing Platform Helicopter (HMS Albion/Bulwark) |
| Make & mend | RN/RM slang for time off |
| MAREN | WRNS attached to a RM unit |
| MM | Military Medal (awarded to other ranks) |
| MC | Military Cross (awarded to officers) |
| MGRM | Major General Royal Marines |
| MOA | Marine Officers Attendant (orderly/batman) |
| MOD | Ministry of Defence |
| MO | Medical Officer (Doctor) |
| MTO | Motor Transport Officer |
| NAFFI | Navy Army Air Force Institution (provides shops, cafes etc.) |
| Nobber | Ineffective marine (useless) |
| NGS | Naval General Service Medal (pre 1963) |
| Noddy | Recruit in the Royal Marines |
| Nutty | Sweets/chocolate/biscuits |
| 'O' Group | Orders Group (meeting/planning) |
| OC | Officer Commanding (small unit e.g. a Company) |
| Ogin | RN/RM slang for the sea. |
| Oppo | Friend |
| PIRA | Provisional IRA |
| Pit | Slang for bed |
| PTI | Physical Training Instructor RM |
| Pussers | Belonging to the Royal Navy |
| PWI | Platoon Weapons Instructor RM |
| QMS | Quartermaster Sergeant RM |
| qt | On the quiet/ an aside |
| Royal | Slang for a Royal Marine |
| RM | Royal Marines |
| RMA | Royal Marines Artillery 'Blue Marines' (Amalgamated June |
| RMLI | Royal Marines Light Infantry 'Red Marines' (1923 |

| | |
|---|---|
| RSM | Regimental Sergeant Major (the most senior NCO) |
| Rupert | Officer in RM |
| Run ashore | To leave barracks or ship, to go out |
| RV | Rendezvous / meeting place |
| R141 | RN/RM Service Record |
| SBA | Sick Berth Attendant RN (male nurse) |
| SBS | Special Boat Service (RM Special Forces) |
| Scribes | Clerk |
| Shake | Wake-up call |
| SITREP | Situation report |
| Skiving | To evade or do nothing |
| SLR | Self-loading rifle (Belgian FN 7.62 model) |
| SNCO | Senior Non Commissioned Officer (Sergeant, Colour Sergeant, QMS, RSM) |
| Squared away | Tidied up |
| Stand easy | Morning break or to relax |
| Sticks | A kneeling line of men |
| SV Boot | Rubber soled commando boot |
| Three Badger | A RM of low rank but of great experience/service |
| TQMS | Technical QMS RM (supplies/stores) |
| USMC | United States Marine Corps |
| Verey pistol | A signal gun, fires red/green/white flares |
| VC | Victoria Cross, highest award for bravery |
| WRNS | Woman's Royal Naval Service |
| Wet | A drink (usually tea or beer) |
| YOs | Young Officers RM (undergoing training) |